TOUGH HANDS

"I tell you there's only one way to do it," Dillingham said. "Hit those nesters hard. Kill some of 'em. Raise hell in general and you've got 'em stopped."

"No, Gene." I brought my rifle around so that it covered him. "There's only one thing that counts with me. That's protecting the Box P."

"But the valley—"

"To hell with it. You think Dodson will turn a hand to help us? He won't, and I don't intend to help him."

His face turned dark red. "Will, you can squat here as long as you want to, but I'm going to do just what I said I—"

"You trying to make me kill you?" I asked. "By God, I will, if you keep pushing me!"

WAYNE D. OVERHOLSER

Twice Winner of the Spur Award
and Winner of
the Lifetime Achievement Award from
the Western Writers of America

WAYNE D. OVERHOLSER

• GUNLOCK •

LEISURE BOOKS   NEW YORK CITY

For Ray Gaulden
In Appreciation of Our
Years of Friendship

A LEISURE BOOK®

July 1992

This edition is reprinted by arrangement with MACMILLAN PUBLISHING COMPANY, a division of Macmillan, Inc. by

Dorchester Publishing Co., Inc.
276 Fifth Avenue
New York, NY 10001

For further information, contact: Macmillan Publishing Co., Inc., a division of Macmillan, Inc., 866 Third Avenue, New York, NY 10022

The name "Leisure Books" and the stylized "L" with design are trademarks of Dorchester Publishing Co., Inc.

Printed in the United States of America.

Chapter One

I saw Joe Pardee die. It was like . . . But how can I tell what it was like?-No man can tell how it would be if a great mountain disappeared within a few seconds, or if the sun that was in the sky one minute was not there the next. Joe had been that kind of man to me as long as I'd known him. I remember that last morning well, even little details that are not important.

When I left the bunkhouse, the sun was just coming up over the Cedar Hills to the east, the sky as blue as I had ever seen it. I washed in the cold water flowing out of the pipe into the horse trough, so cold that, even in early September, it shocked me awake.

I ran a wet hand through my hair, looked at the dark shadows that clung to the Cedar Hills, and then, turning, stared across Easter Valley to the Sangre de Cristo range that pricked the sky with granite peaks. There the early-morning sunlight was sharp and bright on patches of yellow aspen and the dark fingers of spruce that reached to timber line.

I was still standing there, looking at the sunshine, when Gene Dillingham, Joe's other rider, came out of the bunkhouse. He said, "Dreaming again, Will?"

"Guess so," I said.

He sloshed water on his face, shook his head, and muttered, "Must be ice in that spring." Then he looked at me. He had been on the Box P longer than I had. He was thirty-five, a big man who could ride anything with hair and who had more cow savvy than anyone else I knew, virtues which were balanced by a sullen disposition and a mulish stubbornness that made him hard to get along with.

He and I both idolized Joe, but that was about all we had in common. He hated Joe's wife, Sarah, and claimed she was a drag on him because she was confined to a wheel chair by a back injury from a riding accident. It was a stupid reason for hating her, because nothing could be a drag on Joe. He did what he had to do regardless of anyone else's opinion or feelings, even his wife's.

Gene stared at me for a long moment, then wiped a sleeve across his face. "Good day for dying," he said, and swung around and strode toward the kitchen. I followed him, thinking how like him those words were. It pleased him to see men die in front of Joe Pardee's gun. There had been many, right back to the year Joe had built a cabin on the East Fork of Easter Creek and started the Box P.

Today it would be another man, a young fellow named Al Beam. Maybe Beam hoped to cut a new notch on his gun; or maybe he had been hired by that raggle-taggle bunch of farmers camped in the cottonwood grove just above Carlton.

Joe was already seated at the table when Gene and I pulled back our chairs and sat down. He nodded and we nodded back, and he kept on eating. Maria, the Pardees' Mexican housekeeper, brought the coffeepot and filled our cups, plodded back to the stove, and returned with a platter of bacon and flapjacks.

A moment later Dogbone, the Ute kid who did the chores, slipped in and sat down and began to eat. He was eighteen, squat and heavy-featured and greasy-faced like most Utes. Every day I expected him to ride over the hill to the Los Pinos Agency, but Sarah, with her air of calm assurance, told me he never would. He'd worked here since he was fourteen, and he had developed the same blind devotion to Sarah that Dillingham had for Joe.

Sarah did not come to the table for breakfast. She seldom did, although she had made a habit of eating supper with us.

I thought she would be here this morning because she knew about Al Beam. When we were done, Joe rose and wiped the back of a hand across his mouth.

"Saddle up for me, Dogbone," he said. "Wait a minute, Will."

The boy went out with Dillingham. I waited, looking at Joe. Quite a man, I thought. I was proud to work for him. He was forty-one his last birthday, taller even than Gene Dillingham, but not as heavy. With his long bones, long muscles, and thin, dark face, Joe Pardee had been born with a perpetual-motion motor inside that kept driving him from sunup to sundown. Sometimes I wondered if he ever slept.

His eyes narrowed as he looked at me. Usually he spoke right out when he had something on his mind, but now he hesitated, and I wondered. He had never, to my knowledge, admitted he was wrong about anything. It was his gun that had kept Easter Valley open range for the dozen ranches that were here. He never asked for advice; he never listened if anyone offered it. I think it was this hard, one-direction drive more than anything else that had widened the gap between him and Sarah until the fire of their marriage had sputtered out so that now not even a spark of love remained.

He had left her bed after her accident and had never gone back. He offered no excuse or explanation. Joe Pardee never excused or explained anything he did. We assumed it was the fact that Sarah was paralyzed that had driven him to Kathy Morgan, who lived across the creek from Carlton, but I was sure there was more to it than that.

I stood there, waiting for him to speak.

Finally he asked, "What have you heard about this fellow Beam?"

"Nothing," I said. "He's just a drifter, I guess."

"Saddle up," he said abruptly, and swung around and left the kitchen.

As I crossed the yard to the corral, I wondered if that was what he had really meant to ask. The air was warmer, the sun well above the crest of the Cedar Hills, and the shadows were gradually fading. The bright, slanted light on the Sangre de Cristos, too, had lost the sharp tone of early sunrise. In spite of the increasing warmth, I shivered, and quickened my steps across the dusty yard. For the first time since I had started working for Joe Pardee, I was afraid, and I didn't know why.

I saddled my bay gelding and swung up. Dillingham had mounted and was waiting in front of the house. Dogbone stood there, holding the reins of Joe's horse. When I pulled up beside Dillingham, I saw Sarah in her wheel chair on the front porch.

Joe was looking down at her, completely baffled, an expression I seldom saw on his face. Suddenly it occurred to me that there was something queer about this morning, that it was like no other morning that had gone before.

I heard Sarah say very clearly: "You're destroying me, Joe. I know that doesn't make any difference to you, but you're destroying yourself, too. That should make some difference."

He laughed, that great booming laugh I had heard so many times, and said: "I'll never destroy myself, Sarah. And if you're being destroyed, it's you that's doing it, not me."

Dogbone stiffened, his eyes on Joe. Dillingham swore softly; then there was silence except for the thin whisper of leaves above us. Sarah tipped her head back to look at Joe. She said: "I'm warning you. You can't go on killing men just to hold something that doesn't belong to you. You go ahead with this thing you're planning, and I'll leave you."

"Leave me?" He shook his head. "I don't think so. Just how would you make a living?"

"I don't know," she answered. "All I know is I can't go on living like this."

He stooped to kiss her, but she turned her face away. He straightened and laughed again. "All right," he said. "You'd better leave. You know I've got to go on. I can't stand still and I can't go back."

He came off the porch, his face dour; crossing to his horse, he swung into the saddle. I don't think that either Joe or Sarah realized we had heard what they'd said. Once in a while I had heard hard words between them, but never words like this, final words from which there could be no retreating.

We rode away at a gallop. Dogbone stood under the cottonwoods watching us, and Sarah was motionless in her chair, but Joe did not look back at either of them. Presently we slowed down to rock along at a steady ground-eating pace.

I glanced at Joe and saw that his face was as bleak as it had been when he'd stepped off the porch; then I looked ahead at the narrow road that followed the creek, twisting along between the twin rows of willows. I was sick. I, Will Beeson, owed everything to Joe and Sarah Pardee. I had come to the Box P when I was a leggy kid with peach fuzz on my face, an empty belly and pockets that were equally empty. They had taken me in, had given me a job and a home, and I loved them both.

I wasn't like Gene Dillingham, who thought Joe was completely right and Sarah completely wrong. I wasn't like Dogbone, either, who was as loyal to Sarah as a pet hound. I was somewhere between, wanting to help them and not knowing what to do.

When I first came to the Box P, Joe wasn't the aggressive driver he became later. He could stop and plan, and did so at times. He took Sarah to dances in Carlton, to church, to box socials in the schoolhouse, to parties at other ranches, and sometimes there were parties at home. Sarah loved it. She got her deer every fall among the Cedar Hills. She fished East Fork from its head almost to Carlton. She rode a great deal, making a pet of her chestnut mare. She had a flower bed in front of the house, pulling every weed the instant it showed itself.

Now, looking back across the last seven years, I could not put my finger on the day the trouble began, or even why it had begun. It seemed to me that Joe gradually became more domineering and intolerant, and that Sarah didn't laugh as much as she had. She spent more time doing things by herself: fishing and riding alone and working in her flower bed. Then she had the accident, and after that nothing was the same.

The creek dropped into a shallow trough, the ridges on both sides blotting out the far sweep of the grass, and then I saw Carlton ahead of us, a sprawling cluster of houses just below the junction of the East and West forks of Easter Creek.

South of town were the covered wagons, seven of them, belonging to farmers who had left the Arkansas River a week before and made the long pull up Easter Canyon to the valley. They couldn't settle here, and I'm sure they knew it, for Joe's reputation was known miles away. But they had come, staying close to their camp after Joe called on them. Then Al Beam had come and made his challenge.

Now, thinking about him, I decided there was no question about why he was here. A brash kid, he knew it would establish him in business if he killed Joe Pardee, but I figured it was more than that. The farmers must have sent for him and paid him to kill Joe because none of them had either the guts or the gun skill to have any show against him.

I was confused by my own emotions, seeing some truth in Joe's stand and some in Sarah's. He had killed men to hold land which was not his, public domain that legally could be homesteaded. That was theory, any way you looked at it. Actually, farmers could not make a living even on the best land in the valley. It was too high, the growing season too short, the weather too uncertain.

On the other hand, Easter Valley was cattle country, the best. Joe proved that, every fall when we rounded up a herd of steers and drove to Canon City or Leadville and sold at top prices. Joe was practical, all right. To him a gun was an expedient way of settling any question as difficult as this. As far as he was concerned, the law was on the wrong side. He used a gun, and that was the end of it.

There was nothing new about this issue. Still, it was vital to me because it had separated Joe and Sarah. Sarah would do exactly as she had said she would. She had no place to go, and no money; she'd starve, but she'd leave, and Dogbone and Maria would go with her.

If Sarah really loved Joe, she would believe in what he believed, or at least close her eyes to what she considered wrong. That was a wife's duty, it seemed to me. I had never been in love, but I thought I knew how it would be. Many times I had mentally pictured the girl I would love. She was just like Sarah except that she was fifteen years younger and

less inclined to have her own way. If she loved me, she would
do anything for me just as I would for her.

Now the town was directly ahead of us, with a narrow
bridge spanning the creek. Not a word had been spoken since
we left the ranch. Kathy Morgan's house was to our right,
the only house this side of the bridge. She had to live alone.
That had been decided long ago by the virtuous women of
Carlton.

Kathy's place, a white cottage with a picket fence, and
small barn and chicken pen in the back, had always attracted
me. I knew she sold liquor, and I knew she had a poker table
in her front room where men played every Saturday night
until sunup. But I had never been in her house because she
belonged to Joe. To me it was wrong, feeling about Sarah as
I did.

Joe said: "You boys go on. If you see Beam, tell him I'll
be along."

He left us, turning toward Kathy's house. We crossed the
bridge, our horses' hoofs striking the planks with a brittle
sharpness that sounded pistol loud in the morning silence.

Chapter Two

GENE DILLINGHAM AND I DISMOUNTED AND TIED IN FRONT of the livery stable. Carlton wasn't much of a town. It hadn't changed by so much as a building from the first day I saw it seven years ago. Art Delaney's General Store was across the street from us. There was a vacant lot next to it, then the hotel, another empty space, and the church. We had no regular preacher, but one came from Canon City once a month to hold service, and nearly everyone in the valley attended.

On our side of the street was a blacksmith shop beside the livery stable; next to it was a vacant store that had once been occupied by a man foolish enough to think the valley could support two stores, and beyond it the schoolhouse. On to the west were a few houses, most of them small and plain. Delaney's two-story home with its mansard roof was the only one in town that made any attempt to maintain dignity, and it needed a coat of paint.

That was Carlton, strung out along a single street that was often ankle-deep with dust, or deeper still with mud, without sidewalks or lawns or shade trees. As long as cattle held the valley, the town would be no different. About twenty people made their homes there, living, either directly or indirectly, off the surrounding ranches.

Carlton would never be any bigger. Joe Pardee had said that repeatedly, and I believed him. Like a water-soaked sponge, the valley had reached the saturation point and could not give a living to another man. If the valley could not grow, neither could the town.

As I stood beside Dillingham in front of the livery stable, I noticed five men sitting on the benches in front of the store, watching us while they pretended not to. They were strangers, farmers who owned the wagons in the grove. Though I hadn't seen them before, I knew who they were. A farmer in the cattle country always looks like a farmer. The difference between these and the ones who had come and gone was that the others had looked at Joe Pardee, and listened, and left, while these men had looked and listened, and sent for Al Beam.

Suddenly I was mad. Because they had brought in Al Beam, they had caused the final break between Joe and Sarah Pardee. Not intentionally, but they had done so just the same.

Beam was not in sight. He was probably in the hotel waiting for Joe. My anger turned to fury as I thought about it. Joe was risking his life for all the other ranchers in the valley, but the "punkin' rollers" who sat across the street were risking nothing except the money they had paid Al Beam. They were confident that, once Joe Pardee was dead, there would be no trouble. More wagons would grind up Easter Canyon until there wasn't a blade of grass left between the Cedar Hills and the Sangre de Cristo range.

I said, "Let's get them out of here, Gene."

He grinned. "I was thinking the same. I get a bellyache just looking at 'em."

We crossed the street, swaggering a little, I guess. None of them were armed. They got up, scared, but trying to hide it. One of them said: "No trouble now. We're just sitting here."

"Waiting to see the show?" I asked. "Hoping Al Beam will gun Joe Pardee down?"

"All we want is our legal right to—" one of them began.

"Legal right, hell!" I didn't like him. I didn't like any of them. "Either way there'll be a killing, and you'll never get the blood off your hands if you wash every day for a thousand years."

Dillingham had no patience for talk. He motioned toward

the grove. "Git! Pronto! You've got an hour to roll your wheels."

"We've got women and kids—" another began.

"All the more reason to slope out of here," I told him. "You heard what he said. One hour."

They stood there another moment, trying to hold their ground, perhaps not quite sure whether we were bluffing or not. But in the end they didn't have enough nerve to find out. They walked away and disappeared around the corner of the store, shoulders stooped, shambling along.

"Yellow," Dillingham said in disgust. "God-damn' yellow."

I didn't say anything, but it seemed to me that two men with guns on their hips should be able to handle five who didn't. They were just showing a little common sense.

Beam came out of the store and stood looking at us, hands in his pants pockets as he rocked back and forth on his heels. He was young, with a coyote-sharp face and a pitiful hint of mustache that looked like a faint smudge across his upper lip. I noticed his pale blue eyes in particular. Though he appeared to be looking at me, he wasn't. His stare seemed to slip past me.

"Tough hands," he said. "Real tough."

"Tough enough," Dillingham said.

Beam grinned. "Pardee send a couple of boys to do a man's job?"

Dillingham stiffened and got red in the face. I said quickly, "He'll be along."

Beam shrugged, insolent as all hell. "You're lying, mister. By this time I figger he's riding hell-for-leather to fetch the sheriff."

He went past us toward the hotel. Dillingham swung around to watch him, his hand on gun butt. I said, "Ease up, Gene." But he kept his hand on his gun, staring at Beam's back.

From the doorway Delaney said: "Will's right, Gene. Shooting a man in the back isn't Joe Pardee's way."

"That bastard!" Dillingham said. "That long-tongued bastard!"

Beam was inside the hotel then, and Dillingham dropped

his hand. Delaney said: "He claims he's killed twelve men. Pardee will make thirteen. If he does down Pardee, he'll come after you two."

I couldn't figure Delaney out. Most of his customers were ranchers, but he acted as if he'd just as soon see the farmers take the valley as not. In time there would be ten of them to every rancher who was here now, but one customer who could pay his bill was worth ten who couldn't. Delaney was the kind who'd think of that. Still, he favored the farmers without quite coming out and saying so.

He leaned against the door jamb, his eyes swinging from me to Dillingham and back to me. He was a short, fat man, almost bald, with brows so pale he seemed to have none at all. He'd been in Carlton a long time, and he was honest enough, I guess, but I didn't trust him. Joe didn't either. Now I wondered what the farmers and Beam had said to him before Dillingham and I rode into town.

Something was up, I thought. I'd tell Joe about it on our way home. He'd made it plain to the townsmen that they could be loyal to the ranchers or get to hell out of the valley. To Joe Pardee an issue like that was always simple. He never let it get complicated.

Because neither Dillingham nor I wanted to discuss the possibility of Beam smoking Joe down, we said nothing.

Delaney asked, "Where's Pardee?"

"He'll be along," I said.

"He stopped at Kathy Morgan's," Dillingham put in.

Delaney said, smirking, "A marriage vow don't mean nothing to a man like Joe—"

Dillingham lunged at him, a fist swinging up from his knee, but Delaney jumped back and jerked a small pistol out of a back pocket.

"Just like Pardee, ain't you?" Delaney said. "Think you can roll over everybody. Well, you're going to learn you can't. Now get out of here!"

Even a stubborn man like Dillingham doesn't argue with a gun that's lined on his heart. We crossed the street to the livery stable.

"Wait'll I tell Joe about Delaney," Dillingham said. "He won't do no more trading with that son of a bitch."

"Don't tell him 'til it's over," I said.

He gave me a questioning look and let the matter go. We waited for another five minutes, smoking and saying nothing. Why couldn't Joe come and get it over with? Then I heard his horse on the bridge.

A moment later he reined up and dismounted, looking at me. I said, "He's in the hotel."

He nodded, drew his gun, and checked it. Dillingham said: "When we got here there was five plow pushers sitting in front of the store. We gave 'em an hour. If they ain't gone by then, we'll make 'em run so fast their heels will be smoking before they get to the Arkansas."

Joe acted as if he didn't hear. He eased his gun back into the holster, glancing toward the hotel. I had seen the same thing happen before—maybe not in the identical manner, but almost. Joe wasn't a killer in the sense Al Beam was, but he was fast and he was accurate.

I put a hand on his arm. "Joe, let me and Gene handle this. Beam's not fighting for himself. He's got no stake—"

"No."

Joe pulled away, affronted by what I had said; then I met his gaze squarely, and I saw a shadow of fear in his eyes that I had never seen there before. I wondered if it went back to what Sarah had said that morning. One thing was sure: Kathy Morgan hadn't been able to give him any confidence.

He stepped around the horses into the street, and in that same instant Al Beam left the hotel. They faced each other, Joe with the advantage of the sun at his back. They moved slowly, the light very sharp on the gray dust. Joe's shadow moved ahead of him, Beam's behind him.

I saw Beam's face, his features filled with savage hatred that belonged in the jungle, not here on the dusty street of Carlton. He enjoyed the seesaw with death. Joe didn't. Then I wasn't sure of that. Maybe killing grew on a man; and Joe had changed from the husband Sarah had married.

They weren't far apart, close enough so that the man who got off the first shot would be the survivor. Fear grew in me until I was panicky. I whispered, "He overmatched himself, Gene." Dillingham cursed, and pulled his gun, and that was when Beam started his draw.

Joe was as fast as he had ever been, but he wasn't fast enough. There was no question about who fired first. Joe was hammered back on his heels, his shot the result of muscular contraction; then he went down. Dillingham bawled a great yell and ran toward Beam, shooting as he ran. Behind me the liveryman, Slim Reardon, whispered, "By God, he got Joe!"

I started toward where Joe lay, hearing the slamming explosions of Dillingham's gun. Beam may have got off another shot. I'm not sure. He was in the dust before I reached Joe, but still Dillingham wasn't satisfied. He stood over Beam and fired and fired again until his gun was empty. Afterward I heard every bullet had gone into the man's body, five of them.

I knelt beside Joe. Blood showed at the corners of his mouth, then trickled down both sides of his chin. He said, "Will."

"I'm here, Joe."

"Take care of Kathy. I didn't do much for her. Never figured on cashing in. Take care of her, Will."

I said nothing, for I was thinking of Sarah. I loved her as much as I loved Joe. She had looked out for me from the first. Patched my clothes. Nursed me when I was sick. Read aloud to me. Saw that I had something hot to eat if I got in late. Things like that. She must hate Kathy. . . .

Tears ran down my face, for this was the moment when the sun was going down. I thought it wasn't really happening. It had to be a horrible nightmare.

"Will." Joe's right hand came up to feel my face. "Will, are you there? I can't see."

"I'm here."

"Promise me."

I could do nothing else. "I promise," I said.

He died then, his hands turning and going slack in the dust, the palms upward. His head jerked, dropping sideways to rest on one cheek. I got up and looked at Dillingham, who was mouthing one curse after another.

"Them farmers," he said. "Them God-damned, murdering sons of bitches. I'll kill 'em!"

"We gave them an hour." I turned and saw Reardon. "Harness up a team and hook up a rig. We'll take him home."

There were others on the street, but I didn't see them. I couldn't see anything except Joe Pardee's body lying there in the dust, and I wondered what Sarah would do now. And Kathy, what would she do? I didn't see her when we drove past her house a few minutes later, Dillingham riding beside the rig, my horse tied behind.

Once I looked back and saw a dust cloud in the air below town. The farmers were on their way out of the valley, and I was glad. If they had stayed, Gene Dillingham would have killed them.

Chapter Three

EVERYONE IN THE VALLEY CAME TO JOE'S FUNERAL EVEN
Art Delaney and Coley Alton from his trading post at the
mouth of Easter Creek. Yes, and Kathy Morgan. She stood
by herself, away from the others, crying all through the service. Sarah, sitting in her wheel chair at the graveside, didn't
shed a tear. I couldn't tell by looking at her whether she felt
sorrow or not.

Dillingham looked stunned. I suppose I did, too. I was
surprised to find I didn't feel intense grief, although I'm sure
my emotions were not like Sarah's. I had loved Joe Pardee;
I had respected him; yet he wasn't a man whose death brought
piercing sorrow.

I thought about that as the preacher talked, searching my
heart and feeling a little guilty. Joe couldn't have been cen-
sured for any of his killings. The men who had come here
had known the risks they were taking. Unlike the farmers
who hired Al Beam Joe had never dodged an obligation by
hiring someone else to take his place.

He was all man, Joe Pardee. There'd never be another like
him. I hated to think what would happen now as the news of
his death spread. I'd have to carry on his fight. So would
Gene Dillingham, who would probably be foreman. We'd
have to hire another rider, perhaps two, for Joe had been as
good as any two cowhands in the valley.

I was stunned, and I was afraid of the future because I

didn't know what was ahead. But there wasn't even a lump in my throat as the preacher droned on, telling how important it was to repent and be baptized while we were still alive, for we knew not when the Grim Reaper would take us; but I hardly heard him.

I kept turning over in my mind the discovery I'd made about Joe Pardee. With all of his virtues, he lacked one important quality: pity. I'd never given it a thought while he was alive, but now I realized he'd been a hard, driving man suffering from an overpowering sense of duty. Looking back across the years I'd lived here and worked with him, I couldn't remember a time when he had shown genuine sympathy for another man's trouble.

Then I was aware that the service was over and that Dogbone was guiding Sarah's chair down the uneven slope toward the house. Gene Dillingham came to me and said, "Tell the ranchers I want to see them before they go," and hurried past me to Kathy Morgan.

I told them, eleven men ranging from Alec Dodson, whose Anchor was the biggest spread in the country, on down to the little ten-cow poverty outfits in the arid south half of the valley. As I walked beside Dodson toward the corrals, I saw that Dillingham had escorted Kathy to her rig. He gave her a hand up, then stood talking to her for a moment. She nodded, and drove away.

I glanced toward the house just as Dogbone was pushing Sarah's chair up the ramp beside the steps. She had completely ignored Kathy, but that, I told myself, was exactly what Kathy must have expected.

Dodson walked along, his head down, and presently he said: "It'll be hell now. There ain't a man in the valley who can do what Joe done."

"That's right," I said.

We walked across the dusty yard to where the other ranchers stood, the air still and hot, the sun swinging down toward the Sangre de Cristo range. It would soon be lost behind the mountains. We'd had no rain for weeks, and the valley was very dry, the creek so low I couldn't even hear it as we stood waiting for Dillingham.

No one talked. A few rolled cigarettes and lighted them. Some of the women had gone into the house. Others stood talking, occasionally glancing impatiently at their men. Then Dillingham came striding toward us with his rolling, bow-legged walk.

"I won't take more'n a minute, boys," he said. "Just seemed to me we'd best decide something while we're to-gether. It ain't no secret that Joe was responsible for this valley being what it is. Soon as the farmers hear they don't have to buck him no more, they'll be back here by the hundreds."

"I don't think so," Dodson said. "Not till spring, any-how."

Dillingham glowered at him. Though Dodson wasn't an aggressive man, the fact that he owned Anchor made him important, and Dillingham couldn't very well ignore him. Gene said: "I figger we can't take no chances. I ain't a owner, but I reckon the widow'll ask me to rod this outfit, seeing as I've been here a long time and know the way Joe operated; but that ain't the point. Joe done a job. The least we can do is to go on doing it. He was president of the Easter Valley Cattlemen's Association as long as I've been around here. Well, we'd better get another one before something hap-pens."

He looked at the men in front of him, but none of them said what he expected to hear: that he would make a good president. There was an awkward silence. Finally Dodson said: "Looks to me like you're out of line, Gene. The con-stitution and by-laws says the president has got to be an owner. Maybe you'd better buy the Box P from Mrs. Pardee." He cleared his throat, and then added, "We'll meet the first Saturday night of October in the schoolhouse."

He walked toward his rig, calling to his wife. The rest of them scattered in a matter of seconds. Dillingham and I were the only ones left. He was red in the face, and hurt. The corners of his mouth were drawn.

"By God, they'll need me before they're done! They'll find out." He looked at me. "You staying on, Will?"

I said, "Figured I would."

"Then I guess we won't need more'n one other man. I'll ride down to Canon City tomorrow and see who I can pick up."

He swung around and walked toward the house. I started to call to him, to tell him he'd be taking orders from Sarah, not giving them, then decided against it. That was Sarah's job, and I was sure she'd do it.

I walked into the bunkhouse and sat down. I rolled and smoked a cigarette, and stared at the log walls and the pot-bellied stove and the oilcloth-covered table in the back. Again I thought how little real sorrow I felt because Joe was dead. I was bewildered more than anything else, knowing that nothing would be the same again. Not just here on the Box P, but in the whole valley. Dillingham might be right. Maybe the farmers would swarm in like locusts.

Then I wondered if I would stay on. I didn't want to leave Sarah, but I didn't think I could work for Dillingham. He'd be overbearing as well as stubborn; he'd make a show if he had to kill me and Dogbone to do it. I'd wait a few days and see how it went.

Someone came in and I glanced up. It was Ben Sawhill, the Canon City lawyer who handled Joe's legal work, a big, rawboned man who looked more like a farmer than like a lawyer. He was smart and honest, and Joe had always trusted him. Sawhill would do right by Sarah, I thought.

He looked down at me for a moment. He said, "Pretty rough."

"Yeah," I agreed. "I can't get used to it. I mean, I never thought it would happen, and now I'm scared."

"Scared of what?"

"I'm not sure. I guess it's just not knowing what's coming."

"I know one thing that's coming," he said. "Trouble." He shrugged. "Hell, I don't know why I should worry about it." He scratched an ear, frowning at me. "We're reading the will tonight. I've got to get back to Canon City tomorrow. I want you to fetch Kathy Morgan. She's named in the will."

I stood up. "You're crazy, Ben! She wouldn't step into

this house. Sarah wouldn't let her through the door if she did come.''

"Sarah will let her," he said heavily. "I've asked her."

I didn't like it. The more I thought about it, the less I liked it. Finally I said: "Look, Ben. I've got nothing against Kathy. But, damn it, you can't bring her into the same house with Sarah."

"I don't know how you stood on Joe's family trouble," Sawhill said, "but as far as I'm concerned he was an unfeeling son of a bitch and he never deserved a woman as good as Sarah! Kathy Morgan was his kind. But somebody's got to get her here, or at least ask her and hope to hell she won't come."

"All right," I said. "I'll go."

I saddled up and rode to Carlton, wondering about what Sawhill had said. He'd done Joe's legal work and taken his money, but apparently he'd hated him all the time. He was as much on Sarah's side as Dogbone was. I wasn't sure why. Just sympathy, maybe.

Then I began thinking about Gene Dillingham and how he disliked Sarah. He'd give her a hell of a bad time. If she left everything in his hands, they'd get along, but I didn't think she would. I knew I'd have to stay. I'd swallow my pride a dozen times a day. I'd take things off Dillingham I'd never take off any other man; when I remembered the things Sarah had done for me, staying on the Box P was little enough to do for her.

Kathy opened the door the instant I knocked. She motioned toward a chair, her eyes red and swollen. I glanced around the room. A piano, a poker table in one corner, a heating stove, a couch, and a few chairs. Everything was neat and clean, the maroon wallpaper new.

"How will you make out, Kathy?" I asked.

She was a large woman, but shapely, with a pleasant voice and a friendly manner that made her liked by the men who came to her house. Joe hadn't been the only one, but he'd had the right of way. Because he had, I'd heard plenty of grumbling from some of the others in Carlton on Saturday night.

She shook her head at me, unable to smile. A useless question, I thought. She could do a good many things well, including playing poker. I'd heard some grumbling about that, too, and the price of her liquor. She was the kind who'd always make out.

"I'll get along," she said. "I used to, you know. When Sarah Pardee was still his wife. He never came here then."

I didn't want to get into that. I said quickly: "Ben Sawhill sent me to tell you he's reading the will tonight. You're supposed to be there."

She tipped her head back and looked at me, and the hope that she'd say to hell with it vanished at once. There was no shame in her.

She said: "Thank you, Will. I'll be there."

Chapter Four

Supper was a silent meal. Afterward Dogbone wheeled Sarah's chair into the front room, then vanished into the night. The minutes between supper and bedtime, if his chores were done, belonged to him. He spent them in the willows along the creek, or roaming among the cedars on the hill east of the house. None of us knew what he did. He never volunteered anything, and we never pried.

We sat in the front room with the door open, and the chirping of crickets was a steady, cheerful sound. Ben Sawhill sat at the ponderous oak table, some papers spread before him, the light from the tall knobby lamp falling across his face.

Dillingham prowled around the room, his dark face showing the struggle he was having with his temper. He was still angry over the way Dodson and the others had treated him, I thought, and to make it worse, he'd said to Sarah, "Tomorrow I'll ride into Canon City and hire another hand," and she had said sharply, "I'll do the hiring, Gene."

I stood beside the fireplace, an elbow on the mantel, smoking one cigarette after another. I could not keep from staring at Sarah, but she was buried so deeply in her thoughts that she wasn't aware of it.

She never talked much about herself, but I knew she had come to Colorado with her father and mother back in the "Pike's Peak or bust" days. Like most of the others who had come that year, her father had been "busted"; but, unlike most of the others, he hadn't gone back.

Her mother had died the first winter. For several years after that, Sarah had followed her father from one camp to another, living in poverty, working from sunup to sundown, and barely existing. After he died, she had drifted south to Pueblo, then up the Arkansas to Canon City, working in restaurants, sewing, keeping house, anything she could do to live. That was when she met Joe, and I suppose that, for a time at least, ranch life had seemed ideal.

She was thirty-five now, with blue eyes and hair that had turned white after her accident. She had a fine complexion, and I don't think she had a wrinkle anywhere in her face; so, in spite of her white hair, she looked younger than she actually was. Her fingers were long and delicate, and they were always white and soft and clean, for she had nothing to do but knit or sew or read.

When I first knew her, she had a great gift of laughter that showed in her eyes, but it slowly died; and now, as she tipped her head back and stared off into space, her gaze was deadly serious. I wondered what she was thinking about. Kathy Morgan, maybe. I couldn't believe Sarah hated Kathy, or that she was capable of hating anyone. She was a wonderfully good person. I had seen that demonstrated time after time.

It occurred to me that it was a good thing for my peace of mind that Joe was dead. Now I wouldn't have to choose between them. I would have a job on the Box P as long as Sarah owned the ranch. She needed me and I needed her. Perhaps the same thought was in her mind, for suddenly she looked at me and smiled, and started to say something; but before she did we heard the rattle of a rig, and Ben Sawhill said, "There's Kathy."

Dillingham went outside and returned a moment later with Kathy Morgan. Sarah said nothing. She didn't even look at Kathy, who sat down and folded her hands on her lap.

Sawhill picked up a sheet of paper and cleared his throat. None of us moved as we waited for the lawyer to read. He cleared his throat again, and in a clear, slow voice read Joe Pardee's last will and testament.

I wasn't surprised by any part of it. Dillingham and I got $500 apiece, and Kathy $1,000. The rest of the cash, the ranch, the furniture in the house, and the stock all went to Sarah. Watching Kathy's face, I realized she had expected more.

The instant Sawhill finished, Kathy rose. "Is that all?"

"That's all."

"I can go?"

He nodded. For just a moment Kathy's eyes were on Sarah, and Sarah's gaze was on Kathy. That was the only time they indicated they were aware of each other's presence, but neither allowed the slightest hint of her feelings to show in her face.

Kathy turned and walked out. Dillingham would have followed, but Sarah said: "Wait, Gene. Ben can see she gets started." Sawhill followed Kathy outside, and Dillingham stood there, his great legs spread, head tipped forward as he scowled at Sarah.

"The ranch is mine now," Sarah said. "I want both of you to know how it's going to be."

She hesitated, a little afraid of Dillingham, I thought. He shifted his feet, with a sour expression on his face. I guessed he wanted to go home with Kathy, to take Joe's place with her as he hoped to do in the valley. As long as Joe was alive, there'd never been any question of his loyalty, but now that Joe was gone Dillingham was on fire with an ambition I hadn't known he possessed.

"Joe left me the ranch," Sarah went on, "but not his way of looking at things. From now on, the Box P will be run my way, not Joe's. Or yours, Gene. *My way!* That's the first thing I want to make clear. The second is that Will is to be foreman. If you don't feel you can cooperate with him, Gene, saddle up and ride out. Tonight."

This was the last thing I expected. For a moment I stood there and stared at Sarah; then I heard Kathy's rig wheel out of the yard and Sawhill come in. He sensed what had happened, and stood motionless just inside the front door. There was no sound at all. Even the crickets were silent.

Dillingham's dark face turned as pale as it could. He took

a long breath, then asked, "You know what you're doing, Miz Pardee?"

"I know exactly what I'm doing," she said. "Let's be honest, Gene. You've never liked me, and I've never liked you because you believed in everything Joe did. Sometimes I think you are responsible for making Joe what he was."

"I'd be proud if I had been," he said, "but it don't look to me like that's the point. Beeson here ain't dry behind the ears. I know the cattle business, Miz Pardee. I'll keep the Box P going and I'll show a profit. I'll hold your grass. Now that Joe's gone, we'll have to fight for it. If you leave everything to Beeson, you'll be broke in a year."

"Don't argue with me, Gene," she said. "Make up your mind what you want to do."

He didn't answer for a moment. He looked at Sawhill, then drew the makings from his pocket and rolled a smoke, and I could see the pulse beating in his temples. He sealed the cigarette and put it into his mouth. As he reached for a match, he said, "I'll stay," wheeled, and stalked past Sawhill.

When he was gone, the lawyer said: "You're making a mistake, Sarah. You ought to fire him."

"I couldn't, Ben," she said. "I'd have made an outlaw out of him if I'd let him go."

"He'll be an outlaw anyhow," Sawhill said worriedly. "He'll kill Will. Or try. He's staying on just to watch you stump your toe."

"You're exaggerating, Ben," she said. "Anyway, I couldn't do anything else."

Sawhill shrugged. "Well, I've got to get an early start for Canon City in the morning. I'm going to bed."

He picked up the papers from the oak table, nodded at us, and went up the stairs to his room. Sarah said: "Sit down, Will. I didn't ask you if you'd take the job."

"Sure I'll take it. I won't guarantee how much of a ramrod I'll be, but I'll give it a whirl."

I sat down, and Sarah leaned forward, studying me, her hands gripping the arms of her wheel chair. She was a beautiful woman, vibrant and vital, even as an invalid. To me, she was high-grade ore, just as Kathy Morgan was worthless country rock. Then I began to wonder if I should take the job.

There was some of Joe Pardee in me, too, just as there was in Gene Dillingham. No matter how Sarah felt, I had no intention of letting settlers swarm in and steal our grass. Joe had left a heritage that wasn't mentioned in the will, and I would fight for it exactly as Dillingham would. But there was no use borrowing trouble. I told myself that when the time came, if it did, Sarah wouldn't stop me.

"There are a couple of things I want to say," Sarah said. "I'm sure I can trust you. You're the only person I can, outside of Dogbone and María and Ben Sawhill, and they can't do the job that's got to be done. I'm not worried about the ranch. Joe used to say that you had a feel for the cattle business and that one of these days you'd pull out and start your own spread. There's no need for you to. I'll never have any children, so in time the Box P will be yours."

She looked at the floor. "We'd better have an understanding about authority. I won't interfere with you. I mean, if you want to buy a prize bull or sell fifty head of steers, go ahead; but if it's a matter of policy, a big decision, I'll make it."

"Sure, I savvy how it'll be," I said, and lied, because at the time I didn't have a very clear idea of what she meant by policy.

"The second thing concerns who you're going to hire. Gene wanted to go to Canon City. I know you'll have to have one new man, maybe two. But isn't there someone in the valley you can use?"

I thought about it a minute. The bigger outfits like Dodson's Anchor needed every man they had, especially now that it was almost time for roundup. Afterward they would cut down, but that wouldn't help us. There wasn't anyone in town who would do. The only chance was one of the families in the southern end of the valley. They all had greasy-sack spreads, the fathers doing the riding unless the kids were big enough to help out. The only one who had a grown son was Otto King. His oldest boy, Curly, was nineteen or twenty, a harum-scarum kid but a good hand.

I said, "The King boy, maybe."

She nodded. "That's who I had in mind. Take a quarter of beef and go see the Kings first thing in the morning. I'd like to help our own people. Besides, I'm sure we can trust Curly."

I knew what she was getting at. If Dillingham went to Canon City, he'd hire some grub-line rider who might not be worth a damn. Even if he was, his loyalty would be to Dillingham, not to me or Sarah. But he'd have no hold on the King boy.

I said, "All right, I'll take care of it."

I rose, yawning, suddenly realizing I was tired. I hadn't done anything all day—any work, I mean. But burying Joe, going to Kathy's, hearing the will read, knowing that from this night on the welfare of the Box P was my first obligation—well, it had been a full day.

I had started toward the door when Sarah said, "Will." I turned and found her looking at me again with that studying scrutiny I had seen earlier in the evening.

"Will, you don't understand how I felt about Joe, do you? Or why I talked to him that morning the way I did?"

"No, but it's your business, not mine."

"It's yours, too, Will," she said gently. "We've got to understand each other, but I don't feel like talking about it tonight. Later." She touched her lips with the tip of her tongue, clutching the arms of her chair with such intensity that her hands seemed to be frozen there. "Will, he didn't love me when he died, did he?"

She wanted assurance, I thought; she wanted to hold to the memory of something she hadn't possessed for a long time, to dream about it, to remember.

"I wouldn't know anything about it," I lied. "No way for me to know. He never talked to me about you."

I couldn't tell her that, as he lay dying in the dusty street of Carlton, his last thought had been for Kathy, his last request that I look out for her. She smiled a very small smile as she looked at me.

"You know, Joe wasn't a man to attend to paperwork," she said. "He meant to leave Kathy all the money, but he just never got around to changing the will. He told Ben what he wanted done and asked him to draw up a new will, but Ben wouldn't do it, and Joe never bothered to hunt up a new lawyer.''

"He must have loved you," I said, "or he would have changed it.''

I left the room, thinking that what Sarah had said explained why Joe had asked me to look out for Kathy. He meant to see she was taken care of, but he hadn't expected to die, so he hadn't bothered to have a new will drawn up.

The lamp was still burning in the bunkhouse when I went in. Dogbone was asleep but Dillingham was sitting up, cigarette stubs scattered on the floor in front of him. He rose and walked toward me, and I could see I had a fight on my hands. He was ugly mean.

He shoved his face close to mine. "You're scared, Beeson. You're yellow, too. But don't worry. I ain't gonna touch you, but I am gonna tell you I ain't fooled. I know how you sucked around after the widow. That's how you got the job.''

I smelled whisky on his breath, but he was a long way from being drunk. Just mean. I said: "Think what you damn' please, but you'll work for me or you'll get off the Box P. Sarah made that plain.''

"Yeah," he said sullenly. "I heard her. If I was rodding this outfit, I'd handle the valley just like he done, but no, I ain't good enough for the job." He stabbed my chest with a forefinger. "Now I'll tell you something. The minute you let settlers move in on Box P grass, I'll shoot you. By God, I'll shoot you right between the eyes.''

I'd let him call me yellow and say I'd sucked around after Sarah to get the job, and I hadn't done a thing. But to suggest I wouldn't fight for Box P grass was too much.

I hit him, a good one that came up from my knees. He must have seen it coming, but I guess he was too surprised to move. I knocked him down, his head banging the wall as he fell. I thought he'd come up fighting, but he didn't. He lay there, blinking, blood flowing down his chin from a cut lip. Finally he got up and sprawled across his bunk.

I blew out the lamp and went to bed, unable to understand

why Dillingham hadn't fought. I thought: *He's the one who's yellow*. Then I was scared. He was the kind who'd shoot a man in the back. I had worked with him all this time, but I hadn't known that before.

Chapter Five

TWO THINGS HAPPENED THAT FALL WHICH SURPRISED ME Curly King turned out to be one of the best cowhands I ever worked with. He was proud of his job riding for Box P, probably because of the reputation Joe Pardee had given it. His folks were happy about it, too. He gave most of his wages to them, and I suppose it bought new clothes for the little kids, and maybe a new dress for his mother.

The second thing was that I had no trouble with Gene Dillingham after that night when I hit him. He worked hard, and although he wasn't talkative he was as reasonable as he ever was. He was waiting and watching, hoping I'd get my tail in a crack. When I did, he'd give me the toe of his boot.

Alec Dodson was elected president of the Easter Valley Cattlemen's Association. Sarah insisted on going to the meeting. I could have gone and talked if necessary, giving Box P's attitude on anything that came up, but that's all I could have done.

"I'm going," Sarah told me. "This is the first meeting since Joe was killed."

I carried her to the buggy, and when we got to the schoolhouse, I took her inside and set her in the only rocking chair in the building. The men were surprised and disapproving, I think, but they were courteous enough. She was an owner, and there was no way they could keep her out.

I stood beside Sarah's chair, thinking how different this

meeting was from the ones I had attended when Joe was alive. He had dominated the association year after year. Meetings were short and well planned. Everyone knew Joe's attitude on all the issues, and they voted his way; but this time, even after Alec Dodson took the chair, there was a lot of wrangling. The meeting broke up without any positive action being taken.

On our way home, Sarah said thoughtfully: "Take a leader out of a small community like this, and all you get is a bunch of little men trying to be big. Alec Dodson has more cows than Joe ever owned, but that doesn't make him enough of a man to fill Joe's boots."

This was the first time I had heard her speak well of Joe since his death. She stared straight ahead.

The day was cold and raw, with a new frosting of snow on the Sangre de Cristo peaks behind us, and the wind that flowed down the canyons was chill and penetrating. Sarah pulled the collar of her heavy coat up around her neck and then was motionless, her gloved hands folded on her lap.

She was a brave and beautiful woman, I thought, and if her body had not been broken she'd be on her mare running the ranch herself. But now I was all she had, and this first month as foreman was long enough to show me a few of my own shortcomings.

"Will," Sarah said suddenly, "I don't want us to take the attitude Joe did. I mean, to kill men to protect grass that we don't own. On the other hand, there's no sense in having a cattlemen's association if it doesn't have any leadership. You've got to be the leader."

I looked at her again, as surprised as the night she'd said I was to be foreman. She turned her face to me, smiling. I said: "You're dreaming. You can't be a leader if you don't belong, and you can't belong unless you're an owner."

"You'll be half-owner," she said. "I'm going to write to Ben Sawhill tonight. It's only fair that you should work for yourself as well as for me." She glanced at me again, the smile gone. "Sometimes it seems to me you favor Joe enough to be his son. You get a kind of brooding hawk look about your face. If you don't relax, you'll soon be an old man."

I was silent. I know I was worrying too much. About

Dillingham. About the settlers who would storm into the valley in the spring now that Joe was gone. About the price of beef that was down. About almost anything, I guess, that affected the Box P.

I hadn't talked to Sarah about it. I hadn't talked to anyone. But I was plagued by the idea that Joe wasn't dead. I'd wake up at night with the feeling that he'd been talking to me. He'd say: "It's up to you, Will. You'll have to use your gun. I was the dam that kept the flood out. You got the guts it takes to wear my boots?" Or he'd say: "Sarah's soft, Will. You can't be soft and get along in this world. You going to let her make you soft?"

I woke half a dozen times in the middle of the night that first month, sweating, my muscles so tense they ached. Once I found myself sitting up in bed crying out, "Joe? Where are you, Joe?"

Curly King had asked sleepily, "What's biting you, Will?" and I had said, "Nothing," and lain down again. But it was more than nothing. I knew what it was. Too much responsibility in too short a time. And Gene Dillingham was watching me, and waiting.

I didn't know how much difference it would make if I owned half the Box P, but I didn't like the idea. The time would come when I'd have to do what Joe had done if I took Sarah's offer. The locusts would come again, and when they did I would break with Sarah just as Joe had, and over the same issue.

Maybe Sarah knew. She said: "I wasn't fair, pushing you into the foreman's job. If you want to quit . . ."

"No."

"Well, at least I'm going to insist on you being half-owner. If you're bound to kill yourself worrying about the ranch, you should be doing part of it for yourself."

"Suppose something comes up we don't agree on?"

Surprisingly, she laughed, the first time I'd heard her laugh for months. She put a hand on my arm, asking, "You aren't worried about that?" Then she saw the expression on my face and drew her hand back. "All right, Will, it's a fair question and I'll answer it. It was different with Joe and me. The ranch was always his. It was never mine, but it is now. That makes me the senior partner.''

I nodded, for that was right and natural. Sarah would own 51 per cent, I'd have 49. I'd accept it if that was the way she wanted it.

"All right," I said.

"I'll write to Ben Sawhill tonight." She paused, then asked, "When are you starting roundup?"

"First of next week."

"You're driving to Leadville?"

"Yes."

"On your way back, go to Canon City. Bring $500 home. Put the rest in the bank. See Ben while you're in town."

I nodded agreement, and after that we rode in silence.

I had been postponing one unpleasant task, but I made myself attend to it the night before we left for roundup. I had not told Kathy Morgan what Joe had said as he died.

The sun wasn't quite down when I reined up in front of Kathy Morgan's house and went in. People would be watching from the other side of the creek, I thought, and they'd probably think the worst. To hell with them, I told myself, and knocked on the door.

Kathy let me in at once and motioned toward a leather couch, saying, "I'll get you a drink."

I sat down, and she brought a glass and bottle and poured me a stiff drink. She sat in a rocking chair and picked up her sewing from the poker table where she had dropped it when she'd answered the door. She worked on it a minute, then laid it back on the stand.

She sat there, rocking steadily, smiling at me in the thinning light, and I thought Joe must have sat here just like this, feeling the warmth of Kathy's friendship. Who could condemn him? I had, but I could have been wrong about it.

"How are things on the Box P?" she asked.

"All right."

"You may be out a cowhand," she said. "Gene Dillingham thinks he's a stud horse, but if he keeps bothering me I'm going to make a lot of holes in his hide. With buck-shot."

"Want me to talk to him?"

"I can handle him. I can handle any man. It's just that he thinks he's Joe, and he's not."

We were silent until I finished my drink. Then I asked the question I had asked the night I'd come to fetch her to the Box P for the reading of the will. This time there was some sense in asking it. Because Kathy was pretending, at least, to put her old life behind her, the means of support she'd had was lost.

"How will you make out, Kathy?" I asked.

"I've got a cow and my chickens and I had a good garden," she answered. "And Joe left me $1,000. I'll be all right."

"You going to stay here?"

"For a while." She paused, and then added bitterly, "I'm going to stay here long enough to see what happens to the respectable Mrs. Pardee."

I said: "I've got something to tell you. I should have told you before, but I never got around to it."

When I hesitated, she asked, "You don't like me, do you, Will?"

"Sure I like you. It's just that you belonged to Joe."

"I still do, don't I? In your mind."

"I guess so," I said. "It's funny, but Joe's still so much a part of everything that I'm beginning to think he's haunting me."

She rose and came to the couch and sat beside me. "I know, Will, I know. Every night I think I see him and talk to him. Why, sometimes after I've cried myself to sleep at night..." She stopped, her head against the back of the couch, eyes closed. A little later she said, "Tell me what you were going to say."

"The last thing he said to me was, 'Take care of Kathy.' So, if there's anything I can do for you..."

"That was sweet of him," she said, "and exactly like him. I knew he intended to change his will, but I guess he thought he was immortal." She rose and began walking around the room. "Don't worry about me, Will. I'll make out fine. But what about you, living with that bastard Gene Dillingham and Sarah Pardee with her angel-white hair and the Indian kid who'll slip a knife between your ribs someday?''

I got up and walked to the door. "I'll be all right. Sarah is giving me a half-interest in the ranch.''

"Will, don't let her do it." She came to me and put her hands on my shoulders. "I know what she is. I saw what she did to Joe. He had to come to me. I comforted him. I loved him. And all the time that she-devil—'' She shook her head. "You don't believe me, do you? You'll let her buy you, and she'll destroy you just like she destroyed Joe.''

I pulled her hands away from me. I said: "You hate her. All right; go right on hating her all you want to, but don't try to make me hate her, too.''

I left the house and rode home. It was dusk now, with just a bare trace of the sunset above the peaks of the Sangre de Cristo range. In a few minutes it would be completely dark. I thought that Joe Pardee's death was like a sunset, bringing darkness through which each of us who was left behind must feel his own way.

Chapter Six

ROUNDUP WENT AS SMOOTHLY AS IT EVER HAD WHEN JOE was alive. So did the drive of the pool herd to Leadville. When we got back to Alton's Trading Post on the Arkansas, I left the crew and rode downriver to Canon City. I put the money from the sale of the Box P steers in the bank, keeping out the $500 Sarah wanted, then looked up Ben Sawhill.

The lawyer shook hands with me and motioned toward a chair. He asked about the drive, and how the year was going financially; then he asked about Gene Dillingham and Kathy Morgan, and how I liked my job as foreman.

He seemed to run out of questions. He paused, then said: "I told you on the day of Joe's funeral there'd be trouble, and I'm telling you again. Dillingham and Kathy Morgan are the ones who'll make it, but not for quite the same reasons. Dillingham's the kind who never forgets an injury, and his pride was hurt when you got the job he expected. Kathy's different. She hates Sarah enough to wreck the Box P if she could get at Sarah by doing it."

I watched him walk around the room restlessly. He bit off the end of a cigar and lit it, then moved to stand in front of me.

"Will, how do you feel about Sarah?" he demanded. "Do you intend to marry her?"

I stared at him, unable to say anything for a moment. Then I got up and threw my lighted cigarette at a spittoon. I missed, and didn't bother to pick it up. I said: "I ought to knock your Goddamned teeth down your throat. Do you have any idea what Sarah has meant to me since I went there?"

"Sit down, Will," he said gently. "I apologize. You see, I was in love with her before she married Joe. I'm still in love with her. I intend to ask her to marry me after I've waited a decent interval. The only reason I asked was to make sure what your intentions were. She's deeding you half her property. I've been wondering why, but it's her business. I've got the papers ready."

I sat down again. Sawhill walked back to his desk and dropped into his swivel chair.

"Why didn't you marry her?" I asked.

"I was poor, just starting my practice here, so I waited. Joe showed up and rushed her off her feet. You know how he was. Well, they were married before I knew what was happening."

"Did Joe know about you?"

Sawhill shook his head. "No. Neither did Sarah. At least, I never told her." He took the cigar out of his mouth and studied it. "I came close to killing Joe several times. Sometimes I wish I had. He made life hell for her in a lot of ways." He shrugged. "No use digging up old bones. Might as well wind this business up."

He handed me a pen, and I dipped it into a bottle of ink and signed my name. He leaned back in his chair, eyes narrowed. "This may turn out to be a good arrangement. I'll bring Sarah here if she'll have me, and you'll be there on the ranch to run it. You ought to get married, Will. You'd be happier."

"Get married," I said. "Just like that."

I turned toward the door. He said, "Will." I swung back as he rose and walked to me. "Joe taught you a lot of things, including his way of looking at every problem in that simple, tough way he had. It fits Gene Dillingham, but it doesn't fit you. Sooner or later you'll butt head on into a question that will break you and Sarah up unless you see it her way. What will you do?"

"I don't know," I said. "I guess I'll decide when the time comes."

I thought some more about what Sawhill had said as I rode home, a lot more. I wasn't a gun fighter, and I couldn't ask Gene Dillingham to do my fighting for me. But I couldn't sit still and watch our grass go under. There must be some substitute for Joe's gun.

It was dark by the time I reached the Box P and put up my horse. The only substitute I had been able to think of was the Easter Valley Cattlemen's Association. I'd ride over to see Dodson in the morning. There was nothing the law could do. No use going to Sawhill, or the sheriff in Canon City. The association was the only hope we had.

This was early November. As I turned toward the bunkhouse, I felt a few flakes of snow on my face. A storm was overdue, I thought. When I reached the bunkhouse, Curly King said: "Mrs. Pardee wants to see you right away. She's got company. I guess she wants you to meet 'em."

Gene Dillingham was lying on his bunk, propped up on one elbow. He said: "Couple of greenhorns. Been in the valley three, four days."

I changed my shirt. I'd bought a shave before I left Canon City, so I didn't bother with that. Curly, watching me, said: "Wish María'd hurry up with supper. My tapeworm's been hollering for an hour."

I glanced at Dogbone, who was sitting on his bunk, silent as usual. I asked, "Everything all right?"

He nodded. "Sí." He could talk English, but he preferred Spanish. He had been raised around Cimarron, and, like many of the Utes, knew Spanish as well as his native tongue. I combed my hair and started toward the door when we heard María hammering on the triangle.

I walked to the house with Curly. I asked, "How are these greenhorns traveling?"

"Hired a buggy in Canon City," he said.

"Where'd they come from?"

"Dunno. I took care of their team and they went into the house. Been talking to Mrs. Pardee ever since."

I soon had the answer to my question. Sarah introduced

me, and then we sat down at the table. The big one was John Mathers. About forty-five, I judged, a handsome man who impressed me as being honest and forthright. He had a bald spot as big as a silver dollar at the top of his head, tremendous black brows that made his dark eyes look as if they were deeply recessed in his head, and a spade beard with a few white hairs in it.

The other man was Al Romig, thin and dyspeptic-looking, with a yellow-skinned face and dry cough. He toyed with his food, talked very little, and what he did say was usually an echo of what Mathers had just said. The one exception was his remark that he had served with Sherman during the war and that he'd had this cough ever since. He was moving to Colorado in the hope that he could cure it.

Most of the talk at the table was general—about the climate and the resources of the country and what the railroad would do for the interior, once it got through the gorge. I gathered that both Mathers and Romig lived in St. Louis; Mathers owned a hardware store, and Romig worked as a bookkeeper in a factory. I assumed they were looking for some business opportunity. Mathers' wife was dead, but he had one daughter, named Nela. Romig was a bachelor.

Throughout the meal Sarah's face was flushed with excitement. These were the first visitors she'd had since Joe's death, and she'd had very few previously. Joe hadn't encouraged company. "One thing leads to another," he'd say. "First thing you know somebody will like the country and want to settle here. Be a hell of a thing to shoot a man who ate supper with you the night before."

When we finished eating, I would have gone back to the bunkhouse if Sarah hadn't said: "Come into the front room, Will. There are a few things we want to ask you."

Dogbone pushed her wheel chair into the other room, then left, and I threw a couple of pieces of pine on the fire. When I turned, I saw that Mathers was sitting on the couch, his legs stretched out toward the fire. He fumbled in the pocket of his frock coat for a cigar, found it, and lighted it.

"You have a fine place, Mrs. Pardee," he said. "I can

see why you wouldn't want to give it up. But there is no reason for you to."

"Of course not," she said. "Will, they want to know about the land on the other side of town. Between Carlton and Anchor."

I looked at her, then at Mathers, who was puffing away as tranquilly as if he'd asked about elk hunting. Romig, sitting beside Mathers, clasped his hands in front of him and stared at the floor. I brought my gaze back to Sarah. She was tense, and worry lines scarred her forehead. Then I saw the muscle twitching in her left cheek. I hadn't seen it do that since Joe's death. I walked to the couch and looked down at Mathers.

I said: "Mister, you don't want to know about the land in Easter Valley. It's all taken. You and Romig don't have enough guns to steal an acre." I laughed. "You don't look much like farmers to me."

Romig pressed harder against the back of the couch; his face got yellower than ever, and his hands grew white around the knuckles. But Mathers never turned a hair. He said calmly: "I didn't say we were farmers. I asked about the land. Nothing more."

"Why would you want to know about the land if you weren't figuring on farming?"

"Maybe we want to own a cattle ranch."

"That's Anchor grass above town along the creek," I said. "Or their hay meadows. You'll find no open country anywhere in the valley."

"I see." Mathers took his cigar out of his mouth. "I've heard a great deal about Mr. Pardee. How big are your feet, Mr. Beeson? Can you wear his boots?"

"No man can," I said.

"Will," Sarah said, "get that chip off your shoulder. These men are our guests."

"Yours," I said. "Not mine."

"Ours. Or didn't you see Ben Sawhill?"

"I saw him. All right, our guests." I nodded at Mathers. "I'll be gone in the morning when you get up, and you'll be gone by the time I get back. Good night."

I walked out of the room. One glance at Sarah told me she

was angry, as angry as I had ever seen her. Later, when we were alone, I'd hear about it, just as Joe used to. Ben Sawhill had asked me what I would do in a situation like this. I'd decide when the time came, I'd told him; but now the time had come, and I still didn't know.

Chapter Seven

BECAUSE I HAD BUSINESS WITH ALEC DODSON, I LEFT THE Box P before sunup. There were about three inches of snow on the ground, and the wind that howled across the valley was cold and penetrating. Maybe Mathers and Romig would decide the climate was too severe for them. In a steer's eyes, I thought—probably Sarah had told them Easter Valley was just over the ridge from Paradise.

Mathers' presence in the valley bothered me more than it should have, and I wasn't sure why. There was something about the man I couldn't quite put my finger on. He was pleasant enough; he was not arrogant or belligerent; without raising his voice he would be listened to in a crowd, yet I sensed a weakness in him I couldn't identify.

Then, too, I couldn't make an intelligent guess why he wanted to know about the land between Anchor and Carlton. Sarah could, I thought. She would probably welcome him if he settled in the valley. But what would she do if he began to threaten Box P range?

Perhaps things would come to the point where I'd have to defy her. Or go to the law. Maybe call in the sheriff from Canon City. I'd be on safe ground. A judge and jury. Ben Sawhill. The sheriff. Any of them would say I had a right to defend what was mine, and while I was defending it I'd be defending Sarah's half, too, whether she wanted it defended or not.

And then it came to me. I wasn't really worried about defending property that belonged to me, or looking out for Sarah's interest. Back of everything was the memory of Joe Pardee. He'd have killed anyone who settled between Anchor and Carlton, if it went that far. If I didn't take the same stand, the ghost of Joe Pardee would haunt me for the rest of my life.

No, I didn't believe in ghosts, but that was what it amounted to. I was always conscious that everything I did as foreman of the Box P, every decision I made, would have been weighed in Joe Pardee's mind. Above everything else I wanted to think that Joe would have said: "Good work, Will. You did just what I would have done."

Because I'd worked and lived with Joe for seven years, and had come close to worshiping him, I believed in the things he did. He'd molded me into the Will Beeson I was. I couldn't change overnight. Maybe I'd never change, Sarah or no Sarah.

By the time I reached Anchor, my mind was in a turmoil. When I walked into Dodson's living room and stood in front of his fireplace to get warm, I knew I had to have this out with him, to find out how much I could expect from the association.

I'd come to buy a bull. As soon as we finished the dicker, I asked, "Have you met this man Mathers?"

Dodson nodded. "He spent a night here, him and another gent named Al Romig." He lighted his pipe, grinning at me as if he were enjoying a secret joke; then he said: "He wanted to know what the land was like along the creek between Carlton and the Box P. Fine for farming, I told him."

"It isn't funny, Alec," I said. "They were at our place last night, and Mathers was asking about the land between Anchor and Carlton."

My words wiped the grin off his face. He said, "You're bulling me, Will."

"No, I'm not. What's he after, Alec?"

Dodson was staring at me as if he didn't hear what I'd just asked. "My hay meadows are on the creek between here and Carlton. And my winter range. He'd ruin me if he settled there. You know what Joe always said: 'If one of 'em stays, more will come.' " He began walking around the room, then wheeled to face me. "But maybe he decided he liked your side of the valley better. Maybe he'll go south of town and not touch either one of us. Or he might buy a ranch."

"What's the association going to do?" I demanded.

He wiped a hand across his forehead. "Let's face the truth, Will. When Joe was alive, we were more afraid of him than the sodbusters were. It ain't like that now. I won't fight for the Box P and you won't fight for Anchor."

I put on my sheepskin and walked out of the room without a word. I mounted and headed down the creek toward Carlton. Dodson had said exactly what I'd expected him to. Still, I was surprised and shaken when I actually heard it. Everything that Joe had built in the valley had fallen in ruins the instant he died. Much of his strength had been due to the fact that he spoke for the valley. Dodson wouldn't speak at all.

Suppose I spoke up now? I was Sarah's partner. I could belong to the association. I could demand a meeting. I could lay it on the line. If Dodson wouldn't take the lead, then we needed a new president.

I started to turn back to Anchor to talk to Dodson about a meeting, and then I knew that wasn't the way. They'd look at me just as they had at Gene Dillingham the day of the funeral. I was too young, too inexperienced. Joe Pardee could do it, but not Will Beeson.

Well, I could start with Mathers and Romig. I could tell them that if they ever returned to the valley, I'd kill them. If I did, I'd be in position to force Dodson to call a meeting.

I was in front of Kathy Morgan's house when she stepped outside and called to me to come in. I swung off the road and would have tied in front if she hadn't said: "Put your horse in the shed, Will. Come in and eat. You're not going home yet."

Something was up. I put my gelding in the shed, fed him a bait of oats, and went into the house. The kitchen was warm and filled with the smell of frying ham and coffee. Kathy, flushed and sweating, motioned for me to sit at the table.

"You came by at just the right time," she said. "I was hoping you would. I saw you ride past early this morning."

I took a chair, probably the same chair in which Joe had sat many times. During the last six months of his life he had made a habit of eating with Kathy every Saturday night. I shook my head, scowling, and Kathy, bringing a dish of beans to the table, asked, "What's the matter with you?"

"Just thinking about Joe," I said. "This is probably where he sat, wasn't it?"

She put her hands on her hips. "You're a fool, Will. Quit thinking about Joe. You've got a job on your hands and you can't call on him to do it." Finally she sat down and handed a platter of fried ham to me. She asked, "You know these two pilgrims who are in the valley?"

"Mathers and Romig?"

She nodded. "Mathers is the head of a colony of settlers. Next spring he's bringing fifty families to live in the valley."

That was the way she let me have it. Both barrels! I sat there with a filled plate in front of me, my stomach feeling as if I'd swallowed a bushel of rocks. Fifty families? Why, they'd not only take Box P's and Anchor's winter range and hay meadows; they'd swarm all over the heart of the valley.

"How do you know?" I asked.

"Go on and eat," she said irritably. "I'll tell you while you're eating. You don't have much time. No use wasting it sitting there moon-eyed like you're doing."

So I ate, forcing the food down while she talked. Mathers and Romig had ridden past Kathy's house toward town not long after I'd gone by on my way to Anchor. Mathers had been around town for several days, staying at the hotel when he wasn't visiting at one of the ranches. Because Kathy had heard enough about him to be curious, she had walked to the store. Mathers was talking to Art Delaney, and although she hadn't caught all of it she had heard enough to be sure she had it straight.

"Fifty families, Will," she said. "Joe never had more than six or seven to buck at a time."

"He'd have figured out a way to stop them," I said. "Trouble is, it's different now in more ways than one," and I told her about Dodson. "I knew all the time there wasn't any use, but I had to ask him."

"Sure, I knew too," she said. "I've watched Dodson play poker. Joe was the only one who had any guts. The rest were like Dodson. What you do you'll have to do by yourself."

I drank the rest of my coffee and got up. I said, "I didn't see Mathers' rig when I came through town."

"He's finished," she said. "Satisfied himself that this is the place, so he left. You'll probably find him somewhere between Carlton and Alton's Trading Post."

She knew what I'd do. She'd been one jump ahead of me right down the line. I said, "What's it to you?"

"Joe Pardee," she answered. "I can tell you to forget him, but I can't do it myself. That's why I've got to do everything I can to help you keep this bunch out. And there's another thing I haven't told you: Merle Turner is one of Mathers' colonists."

I had walked to the door. Now I turned and looked at Kathy, stunned by what she had just said. Merle Turner was the last man I wanted to see in Easter Valley. He had left the country not long after I had first come here, and I remembered him well: a small man with a disproportionately large head, red-veined eyes, and eyeteeth so long and sharp they reminded you of a boar's tusks.

I remembered something else, too. Turner and Dillingham had been good friends. Now I wondered whether they would resume their friendship if Turner came back to the valley. It would certainly add to my troubles. Turner had no use for me. I remembered why, too, for it was not a thing I'd forget.

At the time Turner had been working for Dodson, but he got into a fight with a man who rode for Irv Costello's Skull outfit, which lay just to the south of us. Merle Turner killed the cowboy, and Joe Pardee decided it was Turner's fault, so Dodson fired him. I had the bad luck to run into Merle that afternoon in Carlton. He picked a fight with me. I guess he thought he could whip me, seeing as I was just a kid, and sort of get even with Joe. It didn't work out because I licked him. Before he left the country, he threatened Dodson and Joe and me. Maybe that was why he'd signed up with Mathers. He couldn't hurt Joe, but he could get at Sarah and the Box P, and Dodson and I were still here.

"How did Mathers get hold of him?" I asked.

"I don't know," Kathy answered, "but I did hear Mathers say that he'd heard about Easter Valley from Turner. That's why he came here."

"Wonder why Turner didn't come with Mathers this trip."

"I don't know that, either, but I can guess. I knew Turner pretty well when he was here. He's the kind who nurses a grudge and never forgets. It's taken him all this time to find a way to get even. Because he didn't know Joe was dead, he probably thought there'd be a fight, and with fifty or more men on his side he could get even with all of you."

"But if he showed up now with Mathers, one of us would get him."

"That's right," she said. "You'd better catch up with Mathers before he gets any farther. Kill him if you have to." She came to me and put her hands on my shoulders. "Will, you can take Joe's place. With me, too, if you want to." She swallowed. "I guess you think I'm no good, but I can't help it. I've just got to do what I can."

I didn't say anything for a while. I wanted her, all right, even knowing what she had been and what she would be again, once she got over Joe's death. Any man would want her, I thought. Her hands were gripping my shoulders with increasing pressure, and her mouth was close to mine. I had to get out of her house. She wasn't for me.

I said: "Sure, Kathy. We've both got to do what we can."

I whirled away from her. "Will," she cried, "didn't you hear what I said? You're not like Gene Dillingham or Dodson or any of the others. I wouldn't treat you like I would them."

I opened the back door and felt the cold wind sweep into the room, and I saw her shiver. I said: "You don't give a damn about me, Kathy. It's all Joe, and I'd know it every time I was with you."

"Would it make any difference?"

"Not with some men," I said, "but it would with me."

I shut the door, crossed the back yard to the shed, untied my horse, and stepped up. Five minutes later I was headed down the creek toward Alton's Trading Post, the wheel tracks of Mathers' rig plain to read in the snow.

Chapter Eight

As I RODE, I THOUGHT ABOUT WHAT WOULD HAPPEN IF Mathers brought fifty families to Easter Valley. Merle Turner had waited a long time for his revenge, but it had been worth waiting for.

I reined up and looked back. Far across the flat the Sangre de Cristo range was a notched wall dividing our basin from the San Luis Valley on the other side. South, beyond the forks of Easter Creek, the land ran on and on until it was swallowed by a horizon made hazy by dust. The snow had not reached that far. It was arid country which held the King ranch and several others. As Curly King often said, no one who lived there needed to worry about having to fight for his land. Mathers or Romig or any man who sought a place to live would not invade that range.

The good land was all at this end of the valley. The Box P formed a big part of it. I was sick with the thought of losing it, not just because it was half mine and because I was foreman of a ranch that had never failed to make a yearly profit, but because it was my home, the only home I could remember with any sense of belonging. I would not give it up. No matter who got hurt or how much blood was shed, *I would not give it up*.

As I rode on down the creek, anger grew in me. No man had a right to invade our valley and destroy our way of life. By the time I caught up with Mathers and Romig just below

Alton's Trading Post, I was ready to kill them on the slightest excuse.

I crowded my horse against the rig, my gun in my hand, calling, "Pull up!"

Mathers stopped at the edge of the road and looked at me. If he saw my agitation, he hid it well. He gave me no greeting; he didn't smile. He simply sat unmoving, the lines gripped in his gloved hands, the collar of his coat turned up, a buffalo robe over his and Romig's lap.

Romig was scared. His yellow face had turned gray and his teeth were chattering, from the cold as well as from fear, I suppose. His hands were under the buffalo robe. He glanced at Mathers, swallowed, then scrounged a little lower under the robe as he said, in a ragged voice: "I've got a gun in my hand, Beeson. Don't shoot or I'll kill you."

I laughed in spite of myself. I was sure he didn't have a gun, and if he had, the chance that he could hit me by shooting through the robe was close to zero.

"Don't count on it, Romig." I nodded at Mathers as I holstered my gun. "I just heard you intend to fetch a bunch of colonists to the valley—about fifty of them, if the yarn I heard was right."

"It's right," Mathers said. "I'm president of the society. Romig is the treasurer. We were sent out as a committee to select a settlement site."

"And you've picked Easter Valley?"

"That's right."

"Why didn't you tell us last night what your intentions were?"

"I told Mrs. Pardee. I saw no reason to tell you."

"I'm half-owner of the Box P and I'm the foreman. That ought to be reason enough."

Mathers shook his head. "You're not in sympathy with what we're trying to do. Mrs. Pardee is. I talked frankly to her, and she gave me some splendid advice. As far as the Box P is concerned, you have nothing to fear."

"The hell we haven't," I said. "You throw fifty families into the valley, and you'll be pushing up the East Fork right into our meadowland and winter range."

Mathers shook his head. "I gave my word to Mrs. Pardee." He leaned forward, gray eyes searching my face. "Beeson, I want no trouble with you or anyone. Believe me. But if there is trouble, we'll handle it. We know the law, and I assure you we will do nothing that isn't legal."

I tapped the butt of my gun. "The law stops at Alton's Trading Post, Mathers. If you go ahead with this, we'll put men at the head of the canyon and shoot the first man and team that comes through it."

"And hang for it."

"Maybe, but that won't help you if you're driving the first wagon. Listen, Mathers. This isn't the place for you. It's cattle country. You'll starve if you try to farm it. It's too high and the growing season's too short. Your crops won't mature."

Mathers shook his head again. "It won't do, Beeson. You and Dodson and the rest are occuping land that belongs to the American people. Thousands of acres for cows and a handful of people when it should be the other way around."

"It's the way nature meant it to be," I said. "You ought to be able to see that."

"Let's go on, John," Romig said. "I'm cold."

"Not yet," Mathers said. "Beeson, Mrs. Pardee says you're an intelligent and reasonable man, but you're neither intelligent nor reasonable as long as you keep trying to impersonate Joe Pardee. You can't go on being led by the dead hand of the past."

"Joe's death doesn't make any difference," I shot back. "We'll fight for what's ours. You and your farmers are going to run up against the same thing you would if Joe was alive. I've ridden a long ways to warn you." I jerked a hand downriver. "Stay out of Easter Valley."

"I haven't said all I want to say," Mathers said. "I suppose you've never lived in a city. I can't describe it to you so you'll know how it is, but it's bad. Bad for kids. Bad for your health, working long hours and barely making enough to live, and breathing all that smoke and stench. That's why we organized the society. We'll bring happiness and peace of mind and health to people who now see no purpose in living."

"You're good with words, Mathers," I said, "but you're a Goddamned dreamer, and it takes more'n dreams to keep fifty families alive. And another thing: Don't believe a word Merle Turner tells you. He's got his own ax to grind, and don't you forget it."

He studied me for a moment, then said sadly: "It happens that I trust Merle Turner. I can see you're not going to be reasonable, Beeson. If you aren't, we'll fight. Some of us will die and so will you, and for nothing. There are too many of us and too few of you, and we'll win. I have always believed that the Lord is on the side of the right. If He is, then He certainly is on our side because we are not satisfied, as you are, to leave life as it is today. We're looking toward tomorrow, a great tomorrow designed for the welfare of people, not of cows. Good day, sir."

Mathers spoke to the team and they went on. I sat my saddle, watching the rig until it disappeared around a bend in the road. I hadn't touched Mathers. He was a dreamer, and a stupid one at that, with no notion whatever of what life in Easter Valley would be for a bunch of greenhorn farmers.

I rode back to Alton's Trading Post, thinking hard. Mathers had been warned. If he came again in the spring, the death of his people would be on his head. I knew what I had to do. I'd stop him. No matter what Sarah said, I'd stop him.

I tied my horse at the rail in front of the trading post and stood there a moment, thinking about what Alec Dodson had said that morning: "I won't fight for the Box P and you won't fight for Anchor."

But we couldn't wait to see who had to fight. Once those fifty families were in the valley, they'd stay; but if we could stop them in the canyon . . .

I went into Alton's place and closed the door behind me. In the summertime I could stand it because the door was always open, but now, in the cold weather, the smell was so bad I wouldn't have come in if I could have helped it.

Alton was about sixty, a stringy man with all his front teeth gone and long hair that he continually brushed back from his forehead. He never took a bath, seldom shaved, and as far as I knew he was wearing the same suit of buckskin he'd worn when I'd come to the country seven years ago.

Alton was not entirely to blame for the smell. The big room was filthy. He bought furs and hides, and often stored them at one end of the room. He kept supplies there, and sometimes his meat spoiled long before he got around to throwing it out.

He lived alone except for a Mexican kid who did the chores and slept in the barn. He had no family, but he was the greediest man I had ever met. He was a coward, and crafty, and his word meant nothing, but I thought I could get him to do what I wanted if I handled him right.

When Alton saw me, he got up from where he had been sitting by a window patching a pair of pants. He said, "What'll you have, Mr. Beeson? Whisky?"

I didn't want a drink. Rotgut was a complimentary word to use for his whisky, but under the circumstances I thought I'd better have a drink. "Sure, Coley," I said, and threw a coin on the bar. "Have one yourself. On me."

"Thank you, Mr. Beeson. Thank you kindly." He got out a bottle and two dirty glasses and poured our drinks. "I was sorry about Mr. Pardee's death. I truly was."

I downed my drink and grabbed the bar for support until the burning sensation eased a little in my mouth and throat and my head cleared. Alton took his drink slowly, as if savoring it. He smacked his lips and drew a dirty sleeve across his liver-brown mouth. "That's good whisky, Mr. Beeson. It truly is."

"I never tasted anything like it," I said.

"You won't. No sir. I make it myself, and I refuse to give my recipe to anyone else." He picked up the bottle. "Have another?"

"No. One's enough, thanks. Coley, you know the two greenhorns who just drove downriver?"

"Why, I wouldn't say I know them," he said cautiously. "They stopped on their way into the valley, and stopped again just now."

"They tell you they'd be back in the spring?"

A crafty expression worked into his faded eyes. He wasn't

sure what I was getting at, but the possibility of making a dollar was never absent from his mind.

"Well, now, Mr. Beeson, I don't just recollect."

"All right, Coley," I said. "This is worth $100 to me if you do what I want you to."

He didn't say anything until he cut off a chew of tobacco from a worn plug and stuffed it into his mouth. He worked on it, eyeing me; then he said: "I'd like to help out, Mr. Beeson. I truly would. But if it ain't legal . . ."

I was angry then. The formality of being legal had never bothered him. "I figure to shoot a few settlers," I said, "but if you don't have the stomach for it you're not my man."

I had started to turn, when he said hastily: "Now don't get your tail up, Mr. Beeson. It's just that I have to be careful."

I laid five gold eagles on the bar. "Coley, if you agree to my proposition, you get this now and the rest in the spring." I waited while he studied the money, the brown spittle running down his gaunt chin. I took my knife out of my pocket and felt the blade. "I've cut a lot of calves with this knife, Coley. If you doublecross me, I'll do the same with you."

He jumped back, his gaze on the knife, then on me, and finally on the money. He whispered: "Mr. Beeson, I wouldn't sell you out. I'm deeply hurt by—"

"Then it's a deal?"

He nodded, and pocketed the money.

"When will Mathers and his bunch be back?"

"The middle of April."

"It's a good day's pull to the valley from here," I said, "so they'll camp on the river. As soon as you see them roll in, you saddle up and get word to me. Not Mrs. Pardee or Dillingham. Me! Savvy?"

"I can't ride that far," he said unhappily. "I truly can't. The doctor in Canon City—"

"Send Pablo then."

He nodded, relieved. "I'll do that."

I fingered the blade of my knife. "If you tell Mathers or any of his outfit that you sent word to me . . ."

"I won't tell them," he said. "I truly promise that I won't."

I closed my knife slowly and slipped it into my pocket; then I put a hand on my gun belt, looking at Alton all the while. I turned and walked out into the cold, sweet air and mounted and rode up the creek.

It was long after dark when I got home. Curly King heard me and came out of the bunkhouse, carrying a lantern. A few snowflakes whirled between us as he approached.

"Say, you made a day of it, Will," he said. "Mrs. Pardee is some worried."

"I'll go see her."

"I'll put your horse up. You best get into the house. She's sure fretful."

"Curly," I said, "suppose a lot of settlers hit the valley next spring. Not just a half dozen like we've had, but say fifty or more. What will your dad and your neighbors do?"

"I dunno, Will," he muttered, and started to lead my horse toward the corral.

I grabbed his arm. "You've got some idea."

In the thin light that came through the smoke-blackened chimney of the lantern, I saw the worry that tightened his boyish face. Finally he said: "I'll help you fight, Will. You can count on me."

"What about your dad and the others?"

He shook his head. "They won't fight. They know they won't have no trouble in their end of the valley. The trouble will be here where there's enough water for irrigation. You know how it is where Dad lives. Not even enough stock water sometimes."

I let him go, then, and turned toward the house. I told myself I'd known all the time that I couldn't count on much help.

When I went into the house, Sarah looked up from her sewing, relief a sudden light in her face. "Will, what have you been doing? I've been worried."

"What could happen to me?" I asked. "Worrying is a bad habit."

"I know," she said. "I'm selfish, I guess. I just don't want to think of what would happen to me if you—" She stopped, biting her lips; then she called, "María, Will's back. Dish up his supper."

I walked past Sarah into the kitchen. I couldn't tell her where I had been and what I had done. The die was cast. I couldn't back away from the job I had assumed. I had made it too plain to Mathers. And I had made a deal with Coley Alton.

Chapter Nine

THE DAY BEFORE CHRISTMAS, SARAH SENT CURLY KING AND me into the Cedar Hills to find a tree. We were glad to be in the saddle. The last few days had been lazy ones with nothing to do except catch up on the odd jobs that had been put aside through the summer and fall months, but for the moment not even the odd jobs bothered us.

So far the winter had been an open one. This twenty-fourth of December was a fine day, the sunlight very sharp on the thin covering of snow. There was no wind to speak of, and although the air was chilly it was not disagreeably so. We climbed steadily, holding to the ridges as much as possible, the snow gradually deepening. I suppose we passed fifty trees, any of which would have satisfied Sarah. The truth was, we didn't want to go back yet.

Near noon we found a cedar we couldn't pass up, a good two feet taller than I was, and as perfectly shaped as it was possible for a tree to be. We dismounted and I cut it down, then we stood staring into the valley, the Box P buildings toy-sized, the houses of Carlton barely visible to us.

I'd never been here before without being pressed for time. Now we just stood and looked, and I suppose Curly was thinking of his family on a greasy-sack spread at the south end of the valley, facing a bleak Christmas. Curly didn't know it yet, but he would be Santa Claus. Tomorrow Sarah would give a $50 bonus to everybody on the Box P, just as Joe had always done, and I'd let Curly go home for a few days. Even at the prices Art Delaney charged, $50 would buy a lot of presents.

For a moment I forgot Curly. Suddenly I was angry, just as I had been the day I'd left Kathy Morgan to find Mathers and Romig. Here was the valley, stretched out before us— our valley, our home—and again I told myself I would not give it up. Then, just as on that other day, I couldn't stand it any longer. I said, "Let's ride," and wheeled toward my horse and mounted. I rode downslope, carrying the tree in front of me, and it took a moment for Curly to catch up.

He asked curiously, "What hit you?"

"Just got to thinking," I said, "about what will happen next spring."

He nodded. "It'll be hell."

I had shaken the snow off the tree, but it was cold and the smell of it was in my nostrils, and now and then, as I leaned forward in the saddle, a branch hit me in the face. Suddenly my anger died. I remembered what the tree stood for; this was the time of year when we should think of peace and good will. .

We put the tree up in a corner of the front room that afternoon. Sarah, sitting in her wheel chair, looked at it for a long time and then turned her radiant face to me.

"It's wonderful, Will," she said. "It's the most wonderful tree I ever saw."

After supper Gene Dillingham left the house, and a few minutes later I heard him ride away. He had been doing so every other night for several weeks. I hadn't asked where he went, and he didn't say anything about it, but I suspected he was visiting Kathy Morgan. That was fine with me. I felt better not to have his great sullen hulk of a body in the same room with me.

We decorated the tree that night with strings of popcorn and paper chains that Sarah had made. She had cut out a big star and painted it red, and I tied it to the very top of the tree. Dogbone stayed in the house and helped us. Though he didn't have the slightest idea what Christmas meant, he enjoyed the activity, and liked to see Sarah happy.

We sat down and admired our work for a while. Then we sang a few carols, or tried to. Sarah was the only one who could really sing. After a time María yawned and said it was past her bedtime. She left the room, and Dogbone and Curly went to the bunkhouse. I would have gone too, if Sarah hadn't said, "Will, please stay."

So I stayed and smoked, sitting on the couch, the fireplace on one side of me, Sarah on the other, the tree in front of me. When I glanced at Sarah, I saw that her gaze was on me, and that the the smile had gone from her lips.

"Will," she said, "this is the time of year when good friends are cherished above everything else. If you have only a few, each means more than when you have hundreds. I can't tell you how grateful I am to know I can leave everything to you, and not worry."

It was a moment before I could speak. "Sarah, you know . . ."

She motioned for me to be silent. "I've got to talk, Will, and this is a good time. I've had this on my mind ever since Joe died, but I've been afraid to say it because of the way you felt about him." She hesitated, then asked, "I can say it, can't I?"

I was afraid to her what she had to say, but I didn't have the heart to say No. I said, "Sure, go ahead," and rolled a cigarette.

"I was in love with Joe and I think he loved me when we were married," she said. "Maybe I imagined it when I married him, because it's natural for a woman to want love. Whether I didn't really understand him or whether he changed is something I'm not sure about. Well, you know how it was, but you'll still think it's terrible for me to say I was glad he was killed." She swallowed. "I was, Will. I was."

I glanced at her and looked away. She was clutching the arms of her chair, her eyes on me, her face very pale. She hurried on. "You never questioned Joe or what he did because you admired him, but he had one quality that made me hate him. He had to control everything. Maybe that was what made him use his gun as often as he did and made him run everything in the valley. I think he actually enjoyed having people afraid of him. Finally I got so I couldn't stand up against him. I simply surrendered and did what he asked. That's why I'm crippled. He made me ride Prince.''

I stared at her, remembering that Joe had sold Prince to Alec Dodson not long after Sarah's accident, but I had never connected the two events before. Prince was a black gelding that had been a bad actor from the day Joe broke him, and only a vicious man would have made a woman get on him.

''He knew I was afraid of Prince,'' she said, ''and it seemed to make him ashamed that I'd be afraid of anything. One morning after you and Gene had left, he sent Dogbone to town for something; then he told me to put on my riding skirt. I thought we were going for a ride, but instead he brought Prince to the front of the house. When I came out, he told me to get on. I refused, and he cursed me and said he'd tie me into the saddle if I didn't try.''

She was staring at me now, her eyes begging me to believe. ''Don't ask me why, Will. I'll never understand it, so I can't explain it to you, but there was something in Joe that kept driving him, kept making him do the things he did. He was a coward. You won't believe that, but it's true. When I came to, he said if I told anybody what had happened he'd say I was a liar. I was supposed to say my mare stumbled and fell with me. I did what he said. At the time I didn't know how badly I was hurt. I was afraid of him, too. After that, he started going to Kathy Morgan, and I was never a wife to him again.''

She was sweating. She wiped her face with a handkerchief as she slumped against the pillow at the back of her chair. She said: ''I had to tell you because it has a lot to do with the way I feel about the valley. When Joe was alive people were afraid of him. Fear is a terrible thing, Will, if you have to live with it day and night. I've watched him bully people into agreeing with him. I've been in meetings when people voted his way because they didn't dare vote any other way.''

I knew that was true. Alec Dodson had said almost the same thing. I had seen it happen too, but I had never held it against Joe. It seemed to me it was natural. Because he was strong, others who were weak bowed to him. Now I saw all of it in a different light. If I had known this when Joe was alive, I would have hated him.

I threw my cigarette into the fireplace and rolled another, only half listening to Sarah as she went on. "Somehow I've got to make up for what Joe did. I wasn't responsible for any of it and I couldn't have prevented it, yet I can't help feeling I have an obligation to everyone he injured. I want people to live in peace and get along with one another. I want friends to come and see me, and I want to see other people. Can you understand that, Will?"

I nodded, and she hurried on. "I've been a prisoner here a long time, and it will be a long time before I can change the feeling that Joe gave them about me and the ranch. We won't fight anybody—not to keep them out of the valley, anyhow." She gripped the arms of her chair again and learned forward. "Will, I'm going to walk again. You'll see."

I got up and looked down at her. "Sarah, I'll do anything I can for you except one thing. I won't give up the Box P. Telling me about Joe didn't change that."

I walked to the front door, and just as I reached it she said, "Will." I looked back, and she said, softly, "Merry Christmas, Will."

I said, "Merry Christmas," and left the house.

After I was in bed, I thought about what Sarah had said. Ben Sawhill must know, or suspect, what had happened that had made Sarah an invalid. It would account for his hatred of Joe. And yet, as I thought about it, I began to wonder. Though I had never known Sarah to lie to me, I found it hard to believe Joe Pardee did what Sarah had said.

I was still awake when Dillingham came in. He stopped beside my bunk and looked down at me. Suddenly my skin was prickly. I didn't have my gun with me, but I promised myself that if I lived through this night I'd never go to bed without it.

I don't know how long he stood there. I could hear his breathing and smell the whisky he had been drinking, and it seemed to me I could even smell the hate he had for me. I wanted to yell at him, to jump out of the bunk and knock him flat on his back as I had once before, but I didn't. If he had a gun in his hand, he might kill me at the first sound or move I made. Finally he went on to his bunk. I lay there, weak and sweating, and thinking that in the morning I would ask Sarah to fire him.

But I didn't. It would have been a sign of weakness that I didn't want Sarah to see, so I said nothing. Right after breakfast she gave $50 to each of us, telling me that mine was being given to the Box P foreman, not her partner. I knew she wanted to give me some sort of present, and she hadn't been able to buy anything herself.

As usual, the gifts we gave her were small. I had bought some Irish lace the last time I had been in Canon City and had saved it for this occasion. It was the sort of thing she liked and could use. She'd make a dress and use the lace for trim.

I don't think I'll ever forget the look I saw on Curly's freckled face as he stared at the five gold eagles in his hand. I said: "Saddle up and ride home, Curly. I'll bet your folks are expecting you."

He left the house on the run, Sarah laughing aloud as her eyes followed him. Ben Sawhill arrived in the middle of the afternoon, bringing Sarah a bottle of perfume. Gene Dillingham had killed a wild turkey the day before, a big gobbler that María cooked. After we had eaten all we could, there was enough left, as Sarah said, "to keep the entire King family for a week."

Dillingham left right after dinner, the hoofs of his horse hammering on the frozen ground until distance muffled them, and then the sound was lost completely. Dogbone drifted out of the house. As I built a fire in the fireplace, I happened to turn and catch the expression on Ben Sawhill's homely face as he looked at Sarah. Because I surmised that this was the night he was going to ask his question, I left the house.

Sawhill rode away early the next morning. I didn't ask what had happened and he volunteered nothing, but from the look of him I knew that Sarah's answer had been No.

Chapter Ten

THE WINTER WAS AN UNUSUALLY MILD ONE. WE HAD A bad storm right after Christmas which Ben Sawhill barely beat into Canon City, a second one the last of March that dumped fifteen inches of snow on the floor of the valley and as much as two feet on the Cedar Hills above the Box P. The March storm was welcome because it gave us moisture we badly needed. With a few spring and summer showers, we would be assured of grass for another year.

We lost no stock because of the weather, but the wolves pulled down two yearling heifers early in March. In many ways Easter Valley was a cowman's paradise. Sustained bad weather was a rare thing. We had no Indian trouble, and we had never been troubled by outlaws or rustlers. Thanks to Joe Pardee, we hadn't been hurt by the nesters.

But all of this was the pattern of the past. As each day brought us closer to the middle of April when Mathers' colony was scheduled to reach the valley, I felt more depressed. This was the year of change; our life here would never be the same again, it seemed.

To make it worse for me, I had no one to talk to. I hadn't seen Kathy Morgan for weeks. Gene Dillingham was the same as he had been, sometimes coolly courteous, sometimes glumly sullen. I was on speaking terms with Alec Dodson and that was all, for he had made it clear more than once that I could expect no help from him or the cattlemen's association. Curly King would listen, but he was only a kid. I was afraid to speak out to him because he might talk out of turn.

Sarah was the one I should have been able to talk with, to tell her all my anxieties and fears. I couldn't even mention it to her; I didn't know what she would do, but I did know what she would think and say. Not once during the winter had she mentioned John Mathers in my hearing, but I usually went to Carlton for the mail and I knew she had received at least two letters from St. Louis, both addressed in a clear, feminine hand.

The tension grew in me day by day until I could hardly eat, and I lay awake on my bunk more hours than I slept. I faced an impossible situation. So did Sarah. She couldn't fire me. She couldn't even get rid of me, now that she had given me half the Box P. On the other hand, I couldn't live on the same ranch with her if I killed Mathers or some of his men.

I knew what must be done: I had to stop Mathers before his colony reached the valley. I kept telling myself that, but what would happen after Mathers was turned back? I didn't even try to guess. I thought only as far as the day the shots would be fired, when men would be killed. Beyond that I could not think at all. I was like a sleepwalker moving toward a wall which barred his passage.

The 14th of April came with patches of snow still lingering in the valley and on the slope above us. There was no word from Coley Alton. I think Sarah was suffering from the uncertainty as much as I was, but she wasn't able to talk about it, either.

Our eyes met briefly after supper that night. I saw the pale, drawn expression on her face as I left the house. My food lay in my stomach as if it were lead.

The fifteenth, and still no word. . . . Then it came, on the night of the sixteenth, some time after midnight. I was awake, my thoughts plodding along the eternal treadmill, when I heard a horse outside. I had kept my gun under my pillow ever since the night Dillingham had stopped beside my bunk. I picked it up and tiptoed to the door and opened it. Someone was dismounting in front of the bunkhouse.

I called, "Who is it?"

"Pablo. Is that you, Señor Beeson?"

It was Coley Alton's Mexican boy, all right. I recognized his voice. "Yeah, it's me," I said.

"Señor Alton, he say tell you they come. Feefty wagons."

I took a long breath, the tension going out of me. I asked, "Are they camped at the trading post?"

"Sí."

"They'll start up the canyon tomorrow?"

"Sí."

"All right, Pablo. Tell your boss I'll be down in a few days and pay him what I owe him."

He wheeled away without another word, his chore finished. I went back inside and woke Curly and Dillingham. We dressed silently in the darkness, pulled on our sheepskins, and took our Winchesters off the wall near the door. As we left the bunkhouse, I wasn't sure whether Dogbone was awake or not. I hoped he wasn't. If he was asleep, he couldn't tell Sarah anything; and the less she knew, the better.

A few minutes later we rode out of the yard and headed northwest toward the valley end of the canyon, the night cold and star-eyed and without a moon. We angled across the low ridges that were the lower slopes of the Cedar Hills. Hours later, with the first opalescent hint of dawn touching the eastern sky, we heard the murmur of the creek, still low because the spring runoff had not started.

None of us had spoken since we left the ranch. Now Dillingham asked, "How are you figuring on handling this, Will?"

"We'll stop at those rocks yonder and leave our horses," I said. "We'll circle them and stay in the brush on the other side until they show up."

"Then what?"

"We'll burn a little powder, and maybe Mathers will decide this climate isn't good for him."

"You think it'll be that easy?"

"We'll find out," I answered.

I knew it wouldn't be that easy, but it would buy time. These pilgrims had come a long ways; they'd be tired and a little shooting ought to scare them. The chances were, Mathers hadn't told them that they'd have to fight. He'd probably repeated what the law said and he would have described the valley, but it wasn't likely he'd told them about me and what I had said to him that day on the river below Alton's Trading Post.

Delay would disorganize them. If I could get a chance to talk to some of them, I could cut the ground out from under Mathers. They'd turn against him and go back. Maybe it wouldn't work that way, but it was the best I could do.

Dillingham said, "I've got a better idea, Will, one that'll work."

"I don't want it, Gene."

"You'll listen!" he said with sudden savagery. "I knew Joe Pardee better than any other man. I know how he thought and what he would have done. He'd have hit 'em at the other end of the canyon before they got started, and he'd have hit 'em hard, so damned hard they'd forget about coming up here."

I ignored him. Probably Joe would have done exactly what Dillingham said. With the odds fifty to three, and with Mathers warned, Joe might have fired from ambush and killed half a dozen men. He'd have cut their hearts out with that first volley. But it would have meant six dead men. . . . Was the valley worth that big a price?

I turned to look at Gene Dillingham's tall, square shape in the saddle, shocked by the thought which had just crossed my mind. Last fall I would have tried to do what Joe would have done, but not now. I'd changed, but I wasn't sure why. Maybe it was the absence of Joe's domineering personality.

There was only one thing I could do and still be able to live with myself. I'd hold the valley without bloodshed if I could, and the way to do that was to throw a little lead close to Mathers' head as soon as he showed up. He'd turn and run if he were driving the first wagon. Any man would.

Now, as we rode in silence, I realized how much I had changed. I was Will Beeson, Box P's foreman, and I wanted to be Will Beeson, not Joe Pardee's shadow trying to make every decision as Joe would have. I was trying to protect the Box P, Sarah's ranch and mine, and that was all.

Ahead of us were the rocks, three tall spires fifty feet high, looming in the early dawn light like ghastly fingers pointing toward Heaven. We swung down and, pulling our Winchesters from the boots, eased around the base of the big rocks. On the creek side was a scattering of boulders where we could find protection. From that spot we could see the sloping trail for a quarter of a mile.

If the colonists were breaking camp right now, the wagons would not come into view until late afternoon. But if Mathers and some of his men rode up the canyon to see if it was open, they would probably be along in an hour or so, and that would be our chance.

We squatted in the brush among the boulders, the creek rolling along within ten feet of us, gathering momentum, it seemed, for the headlong rush it would make down the canyon. The light had thickened until we could see the curve at the end of the quarter-mile stretch of road below us.

Curly said, "Wish we had some coffee."

"So do I," I said.

Silence except for a jay that was squawking in the timber behind us. Then Dillingham said, "Will?"

"Yeah."

"I told you a while ago what Joe would have done. Now I'll tell you what I'm going to do. You're aiming to throw a little lead and scare 'em, but you ain't aiming to drill nobody. That right?"

"That's right," I said.

"Won't work. I tell you there's only one way to do it. Hit 'em hard. Kill some of 'em. Raise hell in general and you've got 'em stopped. I'm going to ride along the east rim of the canyon. I'll wait till the first wagon is below me, then I'll roll a few rocks down on 'em. I'll smash that wagon up and bust the horses to hell. Then I'll shoot the driver of the second wagon, and his horses will get boogered and get tangled up in their harness. By that time the rest of 'em will be backing down the grade as fast as they can roll, and they'll all get into a mess they'll never get out of."

Sure, it would work. If the pilgrims ever did get back to the river with their wagons, they'd have their bellies full and then some. I looked at him, his face shaded because his back was to the sun, but I could see his expression pretty well, the brutality that was there, the anticipation. I thought, This is what he's been waiting for all this time. Then I wondered what would happen if he saw Merle Turner.

"No, Gene." I brought my rifle around so that it covered him. "Joe's dead. There's only one thing that counts with me. That's protecting the Box P. The easiest way to do that is to keep these pilgrims out of the valley. If it doesn't work, we'll fight later, when the first settler rolls his wagon onto Box P grass."

"But the valley—"

"To hell with it. You think Dodson will turn a hand to help us? He won't, and I don't intend to help him."

His face turned dark red. "Will, you can squat here as long as you want to, but I'm going to do just what I said I—"

"You trying to make me kill you?" I asked. "By God, I will, if you keep pushing me!"

He didn't move. Even with my rifle covering him, he didn't so much as blink. He just stared at me, as if trying to decide whether he had a chance if he jumped me. Then it struck me that I had been wrong about him. After I'd knocked him down that night in the bunkhouse and he hadn't got up and fought, I'd decided he was yellow. Now I knew he wasn't. He had been held back by some reason of his own.

Curly King was below us. He held up a hand in a silencing gesture. He said, "Listen."

Dillingham swung away from me. I relaxed, sensing that, for the moment at least, he was willing to let our personal differences stand. Then I heard the horses coming. An instant later half a dozen of them rounded the turn below us, John Mathers in the lead.

"I'll do the shooting," I said.

Outraged, Dillingham cursed me. "They'll run us down. You're yellow. A jellyfish—"

"If he makes a wrong move, Curly," I said, "plug him."

I brought my rifle to my shoulder and squeezed off three shots, the first one close enough to Mathers' head for him to hear it whisper as it went by, the second and third kicking up dust in the road in front of them. Mathers and his men were off the road in a fraction of a minute, seeking shelter in the scrub oak and serviceberry brush that grew in a jungle-like mass between the road and the steep hill west of the creek.

As I lowered the Winchester, Dillingham said harshly: "You could have got all of 'em. Now they'll get us."

I stared at the brush that hid Mathers and his men, knowing it might work out exactly as Dillingham had said.

Chapter Eleven

I EXPECTED MATHERS TO SLIP BACK THROUGH THE BRUSH to the turn in the road and then head for camp. But there were other possibilities, depending upon how much of a fighting man he was. He and his men might worm their way through the brush until they were opposite us, then wade the creek and rush us. Or work their way up the opposite slope until they were high enough to to pick us off.

We had waited about fifteen minutes, my imagination running wild as I considered the various maneuvers Mathers might try, when he stepped out of the brush waving a white rag tied to the end of a stick.

I heard Dillingham cock his rifle. I said, "Ease your hammer down, Gene," and waited until he had; then I shouted at Mathers, "Come on!"

He walked up the middle of the road to us, shoulders back, head high. He showed guts right then, all right. He had no idea what he was walking into because he didn't know whether we would respect a flag of truce. If I hadn't been there, Gene Dillingham would have cut him down. As it was, Dillingham remained motionless, his rifle barrel laid over the boulder in front of him, gaze never leaving Mathers as he strode toward us.

I didn't think Mathers would try to run a sandy on us, but there was no way to be sure. So we waited, with only our heads showing above the boulders, rifles covering Mathers.

The first shot from his men would have brought quick death to him, and he was certainly smart enough to know it.

He stopped on the opposite side of the creek from us, still straight-backed, his head held high and proud. He said: "I want to talk to you, Beeson. Your men can keep me under control, if you're worried."

That irritated me, but he was right. I was worried, and I had reason to be, three of us against his fifty. With Dillingham as wild as he was, and Curly as young as he was . . . I stood up, cuffing my hat back with my left hand, my right wrapped around the handle of my gun.

"You can cross the creek as well as I can," I said. "If I don't watch Dillingham, he'll kill you."

Mathers shrugged, plainly thinking I was lying, and waded the creek. He stopped on the other side of the boulder, his head tipped back. He said: "We're here like I told you we'd be, and you're here trying to kill me like you said you would. Both of us can't win, Beeson."

"I don't figure on you winning," I said. "Take your men back to the river and there will be no more trouble. We could have killed you a while ago, all of you."

His gaze shuttled to Dillingham and back to me. "I'm a little curious why you didn't, feeling the way you do about this."

"I don't want any killing if I can help it," I said. "Those shots were warnings. Now you know what will happen if you bring your wagons up the canyon."

Mathers shook his head. "I have Mrs. Pardee's word that we will not be molested. We were on our way to see her when you shot at us. Does she know you're here?"

"No. This is a man's job."

"Man's?" Mathers said scornfully. "You mean a fool's job. Beeson, listen to me. First, you can't hold us off. If we have to use force, we will. Fifty wagons mean fifty families, some with boys old enough to fight. Most of our men have had war experience. We would be hard to whip even if there were a hundred of you. If I am forced to go back and bring my men up here, I'll put some on each rim and others in the road, and we'll sweep the canyon clean. You'll die, every one of you, and no law officer will touch us because you have no authority or legal right on your side." He shook his head. "No, this is not a man's job you're trying to do. I say you're a damn' fool because you're trying to walk in the steps of a man who was a maniacal killer."

Dillingham straightened, throwing out a big hand toward Mathers. "What are you waiting on, Will? Kill him. God damn him, kill him!"

"Let him talk," I said.

"Are you listening?" Mathers demanded.

"With my ears, not my head," I answered.

"You may be honest, but you're not smart, Beeson.... So you'll stay here and die." He licked his lips, and his gaze lifted to the slope behind me. It occurred to me he didn't believe there were just the three of us. Now he was wondering how many men were hidden among the boulders and scrub oak.

"We'll stay," I said, "but we don't figure on dying. Now, if you've had your say—"

"I'm not done," Mathers said. "I keep reminding myself that Mrs. Pardee told me you are a sensible and reasonable man. When I talked to you last fall, I told you we were looking ahead to a great tomorrow that is to be shaped for the benefit of man. Fifty families will start up the canyon as soon as I get back, Beeson, people who would have gone on living in the stink and smoke and refuse of a great city if I hadn't brought them out there.

"Every man has been carefully picked. Some are farmers. Some are carpenters. Blacksmiths. We have one gunsmith, a teacher, a doctor, a preacher, and a lawyer. We will have a community of our own which will operate on the only premise that will ever bring happiness to mankind. One for all. The profit we make will be shared equally. Nothing extra for me because I happen to lead the colony. Nothing extra for the doctor because he has the most education. The farmer or blacksmith who has no book learning is as important as the lawyer or teacher. We ask just one thing, Beeson, a very simple thing: Let us alone."

"And you called me a fool," I said. "Think a crackpot

scheme like yours will work? Why, it's been tried a thousand times. Think of the early days of the Virginia colony. What happened? They'd have starved if they'd kept on with it. And what about these socialist colonies? They all failed. You claim to be a leader and a smart man, but you haven't got sense enough to know that if a man doesn't work for himself he's not going to work at all.''

"You're wrong," Mathers said hotly. "This plan has never been tried under circumstances like these, with a picked body of men in an area with virgin soil that can be tilled. But you don't have to believe me. I'm not trying to convince you of anything. We just want to be let alone.''

"You're making a hell of a lot of noise for a man who don't want to convince nobody," Dillingham jeered.

"Go back to your camp," I said wearily.

"Why are you fighting us?" Mathers asked.

"I'm half-owner of the Box P. I aim to protect it.''

"You have no need to," he said, his handsome face troubled. "Beeson, I promised Mrs. Pardee that we would not touch an acre of your range. We're settling on the West Fork above Carlton.''

"There isn't room for fifty families on the West Fork," I said. "Besides, what do you think Alec Dodson will do? You're headed for his range.''

"I don't know what he'll do," Mathers said, "but in any case, I see no reason for you to fight his battles.''

"We're fighting our own," I said. "Once you get your roots down—''

"Will!" Curly King was on his feet, a forefinger pointed at a rider on the road south of us. "It's a woman. She just came out of the brush.''

Dillingham swore. I guess we saw her at the same time, a second after Curly pointed at her. Apparently she was one of Mathers' bunch who had slipped past us on the other side of the creek while we were palavering with Mathers.

"Who is she?" I lined my rifle on Mathers. "Where's she going?''

"Don't!" Mathers shouted. He was looking at Gene Dillingham, not at me. "Don't shoot her!''

I wheeled on Dillingham just as his finger was tightening on on the trigger. I knocked the barrel up a split second before he could get a shot off. He might have missed anyhow, for the girl was a long way away, and moving fast; but he might have hit her, too, and that was the worst thing I could think of. I was sore, and scared; too, and in spite of all I could do my voice trembled when I said: "That's the finish for you, Gene. You're fired!"

He tipped his big head forward, scowling. "Sarah will have to say that before I believe it. Besides, you're going to need me. There's just three of us, Mathers. Nobody up there on the hill. Come and get us. You can wipe us out."

"It won't be necessary," Mathers said. "That was my daughter Nela. She's gone after Mrs. Pardee."

He waded back across the creek and strode down the road toward where he had left the others. We might as well go home, I thought miserably. My one great hope had been to hold Mathers in the canyon so that he would have no chance to see or talk to Sarah.

If I had been able to turn Mathers back, I could have faced Sarah and told her what we had done. What could she do then? Fire me? Buy my half of the ranch? No, she could tongue whip me, but she couldn't change what had been done.

Now everything was different. Dogbone would harness the buggy and half kill our team of bays getting Sarah here. I couldn't face her, knowing that the job wasn't done and that in a matter of hours Mathers would be leading his pilgrims up the canyon regardless of us.

"We're going home," I said, and motioned for Dillingham to go ahead of me.

I expected trouble with him, a cursing and maybe a fight, but he was docile enough. Curly glanced at him, and then at me, and I knew he was wondering about Dillingham, too. We mounted and started back the way we had come, a smile on Dillingham's heavy-lipped mouth. I didn't understand it, but I didn't think much about it just then. I was nagged by another thought, one that was far more important than any which concerned Gene Dillingham.

I was a coward. Not physically, but morally. Maybe that

was worse. I knew I was right, but that didn't give me the strength I needed to defy Sarah.

John Mathers would fail. He would bring misery to a lot of people, and by so doing he would hurt the Box P in several ways. It would have been better for everyone concerned if I could have stopped him in the canyon, even if it meant killing, but Sarah wouldn't understand. She would remind me what she had said last fall about making the big decisions. And what could I say to her?

I rode slowly, head down, while the sun rose higher into a clear sky and the day grew steadily warmer. Now, more than ever before, I realized how much the Box P meant to me.

Chapter Twelve

WHEN WE REACHED THE BOX P, I SAW THAT MATHERS' daughter had beaten us. She had pushed her horse hard, and she must have been a good rider. Not knowing the country, she had been forced to take the long way around, following the road through Carlton and up the East Fork. When we pulled up in front of the house, she was standing beside her horse, a tight, defiant smile on her lips as she watched us ride in.

Dogbone had harnessed the bays and hooked them to the buggy. Now he came out of the house, pushing Sarah in her wheel chair across the porch and down the ramp. I stopped beside the buggy, Curly and Dillingham behind me, and waited, not looking at Nela Mathers. She had reason to lord it over me, I thought bitterly. Because of her the colonists had won without firing a shot.

We sat our saddles, motionless, until Dogbone stopped Sarah's chair beside the buggy. I thought Dogbone looked uneasy, but I was never sure what was in the boy's mind behind that greasy brown face.

I forced myself to bring my gaze to Sarah. I had never heard her swear, but I expected her to curse me now, and I certainly expected her face to be dark and lined with fury. It wasn't. She seemed as serene as ever, and when she spoke her voice was soft and courteous.

"Get down and come into the house, Will," she said.

"Curly, take care of Will's horse. Dogbone, you can unhook. I won't be needing the buggy."

I stepped down and handed the reins to Curly. I said: "I fired Gene. He says he's got to hear you say it."

"Then he'll hear me say it," she said crisply. "You're fired, Gene. Pack your war sack, then come to the house and get your time."

He didn't argue; he didn't say a word. He rode to the bunkhouse, smiling again, as if enjoying a secret joke. Then they were gone, just Sarah and the Mathers girl and me remaining in front of the house.

Sarah said: "Will, I want you to meet Nela Mathers. Nela, this is my foreman and partner, Will Beeson."

I was forced to turn to her. She held her hand out, a quick direct motion, and when I extended my hand she gave it a firm grip exactly as a man would have done. She said: "I'm glad to meet you, Mr. Beeson. My father has spoken of you many times."

"I'm not as happy to meet you," I said.

"Will!" Sarah said sharply.

"I've been hoping we could be friends," Nela said.

"You can go back and tell your father he can bring his wagons up the canyon," I said. "He will have no more trouble with the Box P."

She nodded as if that was what she expected to hear. "Thank you. I understand why you aren't exactly happy to meet me."

We were silent for a moment, facing each other. She studied me very carefully, in no way abashed, and despite the fact that I was prepared to hate her I found myself admiring her self-possession and calm courage. Not many city girls could have made the ride she had made this morning.

Nela Mathers was not a beautiful girl, and hardly even a pretty one. She was wearing a dark brown riding skirt, a tan blouse, and a leather jacket, with a broad-brimmed hat that was held in place by a chin strap. She might have passed for a valley ranch woman except for the peeled look of her face. It was more red than tanned, as if she had been on the trail just long enough to get burned by wind and sun.

She was about twenty, I judged, but more mature than most girls of that age, full-bosomed, of average height, and neither too slender nor too heavy. Her eyes were gray, her hair dark brown, her chin square and strong.

A man could see these things in one glance, but there was more to her than that, more than a man would see in a thousand glances. I brought my gaze to Sarah's face, and looked back at Nela Mathers the next second, my eyes pulled there by some force which I did not understand.

"Will you come in, Nela?" Sarah asked.

"No, thank you. Dad will be worried about me. He'll want to hear what Mr. Beeson just said, about not having any more trouble."

She turned to her horse, and I gave her a hand up. When she was in the saddle, I said, "You ride well."

"Thank you." She leaned forward, her gray eyes meeting mine. "Mr. Beeson, we don't want to fight with you. Will you come to see us, please, just as soon as we're settled?"

"I expect to," I said. "You told me your father had spoken of me. What did he say?"

For the first time she seemed embarrassed. "He said you were a strong-minded young man who was so certain you were right that you would make mistakes." The smile that touched her lips lighted her entire face. "We're strong-minded too, my father and I, but we still want to be friends."

I shook my head at her. "Not if you're going to plow our grass under. No people can be friends if one is determined to destroy the other."

"We're not going to destroy you," she said sharply. "Mrs. Pardee understands. All we want is a place to live. That will be on the other side of the valley. It won't concern you in the least."

"It will concern me because you'll fail," I said. "This isn't farming country and it never will be. After you fail, some of your people will spread out. They'll want our water and our land, but if they try to take it I'll try to kill them and they'll try to kill me."

Nela looked at Sarah. "Dad's right. You can't argue with him. Good day, Mrs. Pardee."

She rode away, back down the road toward Carlton. Watching her, I felt a stirring of interest I had never felt for another woman. I sensed that she possessed the tough-fibered courage a person needed to conquer this country and live here. She would survive, I thought, when the rest had failed and moved on. I was surprised to find myself regretting that destiny had rigged the game so that she was on the other side of the fence and we could never be friends.

"Roll me back into the house, Will," Sarah said.

I had never heard her voice tremble so with emotion. When I looked at her, I saw she was crying. I wheeled her across the yard and up the ramp into the house.

"Will," she whispered, "put me on the couch."

I lifted her from her wheel chair, her hands clutching me as if afraid I would let her fall. When I placed her on the couch, she gripped my arm and pulled me down beside her. I thought how light she was, how thin her arms and legs were; and I found it hard to believe she was the same woman who used to fish the length of East Fork and get her deer every fall and spend hours working in her garden and flower beds.

Then I remembered that at Christmas she had told me she would walk again. I half believed she would. Sarah Pardee had been a fighter, and she would go right on fighting as long as she was alive.

Sarah wasn't crying now. She stared at me for a long moment, and then said: "It would be no use to remind you what I've done for you. You could balance it all off with things you've done for me. That's fair enough. But I thought we understood each other. I tried to make it clear because I didn't want this to happen." She swallowed. "Why did you do it, Will?"

I couldn't sit there beside her. I pulled loose from her grip and began walking around the room, my heart pounding, my throat tightening so I couldn't swallow. At that moment I wished I was a child again and could cry and find relief from tension in tears.

I came back to her. I had to say something, had to make her understand; but the words wouldn't come. I wiped my hand across my face, and it came away wet with sweat.

"We should have talked about it before," Sarah said, "but I thought I'd told you enough. About Joe, I mean, and . . ."

"Sarah, Joe had nothing to do with it. I'm not trying to wear his boots. We could have killed a bunch of them this morning. They were all in the open, six of them. I think Joe would have done it, but I couldn't."

"Oh, Will, I'm glad of that! But why did you—"

"Listen, Sarah." I sat down beside her again and took her hands. "I know what you've done for me. Whatever I've done for you will never come within a mile of balancing what I owe you. I did what I did because I owe you so much, and because I've got a home I don't want to lose. Mathers is wrong. They're all wrong. You know that, Sarah. You know what will happen when they try to farm the land."

"But it's their right to try, Will," she said. "We can't go on keeping people out of the valley. That was what Joe did, and it's what you're trying to do. Can't you see how wrong it is? They're here. Maybe John Mathers will fail, and maybe the dream he has will turn into a nightmare, but they've got the right to try."

I was silent. She was right, according to her convictions, but I was right too, according to mine, and what could you do about a situation like that? Here was one of the differences between Joe Pardee and me. He would never have admitted that Sarah was right by any standard.

Finally I said: "I came back this morning because I knew how you would take it, and I don't have enough courage to fight you about it. I agreed that you could make the big decisions. Well, you've made this one."

She smiled faintly. "The day will come when you'll thank me for it because you will have nothing to regret."

I couldn't agree to that, of course, but I let it go. "I don't want to hurt you—not ever—but I won't let them have our grass. If they come, I'll kill them."

Her fingers fluttered on her lap, her pulse hammered in her temple, and her voice was very low when she said, "I couldn't have stood it if you had killed John Mathers or some of his men."

"I may have to kill some of them yet," I said, "if they try to steal our grass."

"But they won't!" she cried. "I've told you they won't. They're going to buy Anchor from Alec Dodson."

"They're loco," I said. "Alec won't sell."

"He'll sell, all right. John Mathers sized him up as a weak man. He is, Will. You know he is."

"Not that weak. Sarah, Mathers is a crazy idealist. I tell you, before he's done he'll bring misery to the whole valley."

She shook her head. "No, he'll bring happiness. He has a wonderful dream, Will. We can't turn against a man because he's an idealist."

"He could take his dream somewhere else," I said.

"You had your chance to make him take it somewhere else." It was Gene Dillingham, standing in the doorway, his hands shoved under his waistband. "Now it's too late. I'll take my time, Miz Pardee."

"Put me into my chair, Will," she said. "I'll get it."

I obeyed, and she wheeled herself into her bedroom. I stood facing Dillingham, hearing the steady ticking of the tall pendulum clock in the corner of the room. He was breathing hard, his big face twisted with hatred of me.

Sarah returned with his pay, and as he pocketed it the smile returned to his lips. He took off his gun belt and laid it on the porch. Then he said: "I've had the short end of the stick from the day Joe died. Now I'm gonna give it back. Take off your gun, Beeson."

Now I understood why he hadn't fought the time I had knocked him down, and why he'd stood beside my bunk in the darkness, hating me and wanting to kill me, but keeping himself under control. As long as he had a job on the Box P, there was a chance he would eventually become foreman. He had been that sure I'd fail.

Now he would never walk in the footsteps of Joe Pardee, and that was what he had wanted above all other things. I had fired him this morning, but he wouldn't believe it until he heard Sarah say the words, and he had grinned because he was thinking then that he would beat me until I was dead, or never able to ride again.

There was a moment of terrible silence; then Sarah understood, and she cried out, "No, Will! Get out of here, Gene!"

But Gene's challenge I could not avoid, not even for Sarah. I took off my gun belt, laid it on the couch, and walked toward the door, Dillingham backing away until he was off the porch. He did not stop until he was on the other side of the cottonwoods; then he spit on his hands, a grin distorting his thick lips as he said, "All right, Beeson. Now we'll see."

Chapter Thirteen

I WAS SCARED AS I WALKED ACROSS THE YARD TO WHERE Dillingham waited. I would be a liar if I said anything else. But it wasn't the kind of fear I'd felt that morning when I saw Nela Mathers get away and knew I must face Sarah with the job I had set out to do not done at all. I'd had a sense of hopelessness then, of absolute frustration, but not now. I could do something about this.

Sarah sat in her wheel chair behind me. Dogbone and Curly King were standing beside the corral gate. Now, apparently realizing what was happening, they started toward us.

Suddenly I felt good. I hated Gene Dillingham. I had every reason to hate him. A flash of memory reminded me of a dozen indignities I had suffered at his hands, particularly when I first came to the Box P. I was smaller, and younger, and therefore fair game for a man like Gene Dillingham. Joe Pardee let us strictly alone. A boy had to grow up to be tough enough to stand on his two feet, or go under. If he went under, Joe had no respect for him. The fact that I had survived was one reason Joe had liked and trusted me.

Gene Dillingham had reason to hate me, too. He was probably jealous of me as he had been jealous of everyone who had meant anything to Joe. But it must have been far worse after Joe's death when Alec Dodson and the other ranchers had shoved him aside as if he were of no consequence; then Sarah had made me foreman and half-owner of the ranch. He was not a man who could swallow his pride, so he had waited, hoping he would have the satisfaction of seeing me fail. But I hadn't, and now this was all that was left.

We were twenty feet apart when he ran toward me. I stopped, my fists cocked in front of my face. He started a blow from his knees, but missed and swung off balance. I caught him squarely on the point of his jaw and knocked him flat on his back.

After that I was a little crazy. Landing the first blow gave me an advantage, and I could not afford to let up. Dillingham would kill me if he could, or break an arm, or gouge my eyes out. Because I couldn't let any of those things happen, I was an animal, fighting like an animal, without rules, without any sense of sportsmanship or decency. I wanted to live.

Dillingham got to his hands and knees, a little dazed. I kicked him in the face, knocking his head up, and he fell sideways. I jumped on him, my knees thudding into his belly, and I hit him with my fists, anywhere I could and as often as I could, driven by the knowledge that he was bigger than I was, and stronger, and that I had to win now if I won at all.

I hurt him at the start, and slowed him up. Even then, he came close to finishing me. He got his arms around me and squeezed, smothering my blows so that they had no authority. I thought that my lungs would explode and that he was going to break every rib in my body.

From a long way off I heard Curly's yell: "Bust out of it, Will! Bust out of it!" I squirmed and twisted, using my elbows and fists and boots, but I accomplished nothing. We rolled over and over on the ground, dust rising around us in a thick cloud.

I couldn't break out of his grip. He was too strong, too heavy. He wasn't trying to hit me. He was willing to take any punishment I could give him, which wasn't much. We rolled over again until I was on top. I slammed my head down as hard as I could. I got him on the nose and flattened it and brought a gush of blood. His grip went slack, just for a moment, but long enough for me to break loose.

I rose to my feet and backed away, trying to get my breath.

He'd have had me if he'd held on another ten seconds, and I think he knew it. He was on his feet at once, spat out a mouthful of blood, and rushed me. I kept backing up, still laboring for breath, but it seemed a long time before I got it. During that time I did nothing except duck and block his blows if I could, and keep going back. He got one through to the side of my face and I went down, but I was up again before he could fall on me.

I was tired and sick and hurt, and for several tortured seconds I wasn't sure I could stay on my feet. But he was hurt too. Blood flowed from his battered nose in a steady stream. Still he kept pushing and I kept retreating. I took no chances until I had my wind back. That was where he made his mistake. He thought I was hurt worse than I was.

I reversed my tactics, suddenly and without warning, and stood my ground. I hit him solidly on the side of the head, a little too high to flatten him; I nailed him in the stomach with my left. I smashed through his guard to his face again and knocked him back on his heels, but only for a moment; then he had his balance, and we stood that way, swinging as hard as we could, getting hit in order to hit.

He slammed a right to my jaw that almost finished me. If he had landed it in the first of the fight, he'd have knocked me cold, but now much of the steam was gone from his punches. Still, it started the ground to spinning and I went back again, intent only on staying on my feet. Then my head cleared and we were at it again.

I was so tired that it was a great effort to swing a fist. Then my numbed brain realized that he was as badly off as I was. We had fought ourselves into a state of exhaustion, our faces masses of cuts and bruises. My left eye was closed. Both of his were puffy.

Suddenly I stepped back. He held his fists in front of his face and shoved his head forward, peering as if trying to find me. I came in, as fast as I could, but I suppose I was actually slow; I cracked him on the jaw and he went down, slowly, sort of rocking forward, and fell on his face. I backed up and stood against a cottonwood, the sound of my breathing an ugly rasping noise to my own ears, so tired I could not have stood up by myself.

"Come here and get his gun, Dogbone," Sarah called. "Bring his horse, Curly. Lift him into the saddle. Don't ever come back, Gene! Do you hear?"

Only then did I realize he had not been knocked out. I just hadn't hit him hard enough. I was too far gone to have the strength. His hatred and desire to hammer me into blood pulp were not enough to keep him fighting. He'd quit.

He got to his hands and knees and stared at the house, trying to see Sarah. Dogbone came with the gun belt and wrapped it around the saddle horn. Together Curly and the Ute boy got him into the saddle.

He left, riding like a sack of wool, almost falling out of the saddle at times; and it came to me that it was not over and that it would not be over until Gene Dillingham was dead. That was the last thing I remembered clearly. My knees were rubber. Now they gave and I slid to the ground, the bark of the tree raking my back as I fought to hold myself upright, and failed.

When I came to, I was in bed in the house, in the room Joe Pardee had occupied from the time Sarah hurt her back until his death. My body was one great ache. I could not take a deep breath. One eye was still swollen shut. As I lay on my back and thought about it, I wasn't sure I had actually whipped Dillingham. Or if I had, it had been by a very small margin.

"Will."

I had not realized until then that Sarah was sitting beside me. Slowly and painfully I turned my head. She had been crying again.

"Is it bad, Will?"

"No."

"I should have fired him the day I made you foreman," she said sadly. "Ben Sawhill was right. I was afraid I'd make an outlaw out of him, but he's an outlaw now, isn't he?"

"Yes."

I wondered what would happen to Gene Dillingham. I wished he was dead. He was not a man to forget he had been humiliated. He would strike back at me or at Sarah, or both of us. If he picked up his friendship with Merle Turner again, he might even throw in with the colonists.

Sarah was silent for a moment; then she said: "Will, just make one promise. Try to get along with John Mathers. Is that too much to ask?"

I looked at her with my one good eye. The slanting sunlight of late afternoon was falling through the lace curtain that covered the window. I had never seen her more beautiful than she was at that moment. I wondered if it was the thought of Mathers that made her look that way. Perhaps she had seen something in Mathers that attracted her.

"No, it isn't too much. I'll try." I started to get up, but fell back as pain racked me. "Damn it, I . . ."

"What are you trying to get up for?"

"There's work to be done."

"Nothing that's urgent."

"Calves to brand."

She smiled. "They'll be here when you're able to get up. Now, you get some sleep."

She wheeled herself out of the room. I wouldn't sleep, I thought. I'd lie here and torture myself wondering what Gene Dillingham would do. And Merle Turner. And how far Sarah would go to please John Mathers. And how long it would take the colonists to overrun Box P range.

I'd see Alec Dodson as soon as I was able to ride. If he was scared enough, he might sell. A pretty weak reed, I thought. Damn it, I should have defied Sarah and kept Mathers bottled up in the canyon.

I was sick with regret, for now there was nothing I could do.

Chapter Fourteen

A WEEK PASSED BEFORE I RODE TO ANCHOR, AND EVEN after all that time my left eye was a great purple patch, and every deep breath sent a flash of pain through me that almost doubled me up. I didn't feel much like riding, but I had to find another man to replace Dillingham, and I was determined to see Alec Dodson again.

When I rode through Carlton, Art Delaney was sweeping off the walk in front of his store. He waved a fat hand. "Haven't seen you for quite a spell, Will. Where you been?"

"Home." I reined up across the hitch pole from him. "Haven't felt like sashaying around."

"Dillingham?" I nodded, and he said: "Must have been some ruckus. He looks twice as bad as you do."

"Know where I can find a good cowhand?"

"Might get one of Alec Dodson's boys." He scratched his head, grinning maliciously. "Well, sir, looks like the ghost of Joe Pardee is about to be laid to rest."

I said, "I guess you kind o' cotton to this colony bunch."

"Why not? I was getting damned sick of Pardee's talk about how the valley was supporting everybody it could."

I rode on. If I hadn't, I'd have got off my horse and given Delaney a whipping. Better wait and ride it out, I thought.

The first wagon of the colonists had been pulled into the

willows along the creek not more than fifty yards beyond Carlton. A woman wearing a faded calico dress and sunbonnet bent over a washtub. Three children played in the shallow water along the edge of the stream, but the man and his horses were not in sight.

I pulled off the road and made a circle through the hills to Anchor, adding an hour to my time, but I preferred that to riding past fifty wagons. I didn't want to see Mathers or his girl or any of them. There would be trouble if I saw them today, with the mood I was in, and I didn't want trouble right now.

When I reached Anchor, Dodson was sitting on a sawhorse in front of his house whittling on a piece of cedar. I said, "Howdy, Alec." He looked up but didn't speak. His face was as gray as death. He lowered his head and went on whittling.

"The locusts have moved in," I said.

He jumped up, threw the cedar stick to the ground, and jammed his knife into his pocket. "Yeah, yeah," he said, and started for his house.

There was no sense in his acting that way with me. I spurred my horse forward and cut him off from the house. "What the hell's the matter with you?" I said.

He stared at me, tears rolling down his face. "You can see what's the matter without asking." He choked and wiped a hand across his eyes. "Blubbering like a damned woman." He turned and pointed down the creek, the white tops of twenty or more of the wagons visible from where we were. "All I've got left is this quarter-section." He swallowed and wiped his eyes again. "If Joe was alive, they wouldn't be here. You're Box P. Why didn't you keep 'em out of the valley?"

"Why, God damn you," I said. "You're president of the cattlemen's association. Call a meeting. Call it for tonight. Send your boys out to every ranch in the valley."

"No," he said. "I'll never call a meeting."

He started around my horse toward the house. I said: "I fired Dillingham. Got a man you can spare?"

He stopped. "Who do you want?"

His men were all good hands, but I knew Red Thurston better than the others, so I said, "Red," and he nodded. "I'll send him over in a few days," he said, and went on into the house.

I rode away, not understanding why Dodson had acted the way he had. More than once during the winter we'd had hard words over what the cattlemen's association could and should do. Once I had even gone over his head and talked to the members individually in hopes of working out a plan on which we could agree. Dodson hadn't liked it and he'd told me so, but our difference had never gone beyond words. He didn't have any reason to treat me as if I were poison, or blame me for letting the colonists into the valley.

Again I circled the wagons, striking the road just above Carlton. As I passed the store, I suddenly remembered that Delaney had said I might get one of Dodson's boys. I wondered how he knew.

When I reached Kathy Morgan's house, she was standing at the front gate. She smiled, calling: "Come in for a minute, Will. I'll give you a drink."

I said, "All right. It's time I was looking at a friendly face. I just came from Anchor."

"How's Alec?"

"Crazy," I said. "Crazy as a loon." I tied my horse and stepped through the gate. She took my arm as we walked to the house, and I told her what happened. "And he wants to know why I didn't keep them out of the valley."

"That's like him," she said.

We went in, and she motioned for me to sit down. "I'll get your drink," she said, and disappeared into the kitchen.

I leaned my head against the back of the leather chair. To hell with it, I told myself. From now on my worries were going to be strictly Box P business.

Kathy returned a moment later and handed me a glass of whisky. I drank it, feeling its warmth work through me. We were silent for a time, and it seemed to me that Joe Pardee was gone from our lives; yet it had been only a short time ago that Kathy and I had sat here just as we were now, both of us saying Joe was haunting us.

That was one of the great gifts of time, this healing and forgetting. I started to say something like that to Kathy; then I looked at her, and decided against it. I had a feeling that Joe's death was not forgotten, that the wound had not yet healed.

She said petulantly: "You've treated me badly, Will. You haven't been here for months."

"No point in my coming here," I said. "I told you that. Joe would always be between us."

"No, Will, no!" she cried. "I need a man—I need you. There's so much of Joe in you."

"No," I said. "I'm just Will Beeson, and that's all I want to be."

Quick fury touched her face. "That's some of the widow's work. She's bought you, Will, with half a ranch. It's a cheap price for a man. I warned you about it. I know what she wants and how she goes about getting it. I know every Goddamned thought that goes through her warped little brain—"

"Kathy!" I got up. "I told you once that you could hate her for all you're worth, but don't try to make me hate her, too."

"I'm sorry, Will," she said then. "I didn't mean to say all of that. It just came out because I expected so much from you and you haven't done the job you could have. I know what happened that morning when Mathers was coming up the canyon. You could have stopped them then, but you missed your chance. And why? Because Sarah has you wound around her little finger. Everybody in the valley knows it but you. She names the song and you sing it. That's right, isn't it?"

I dropped back into the chair again. "Gene Dillingham's been here, hasn't he?"

"No," she said impatiently. "I heard about it in the store. Gene probably told it to Delaney or in the blacksmith shop or stable. Anyhow, it's all over the valley, how you had Mathers stopped; but you let his girl slip past, and because you knew she was going after Sarah, you quit. Partners!"

Kathy laughed scornfully. "Why, you're nothing but a hired hand, Will."

For a moment I was angry. Then I wanted to laugh, but I didn't. I said, "All right, maybe you can tell me what to do now."

"Sure I can," she said. "There's only one thing that can whip as many as we've got in the valley. That's the climate. Everything's wonderful with them now—big hopes and dreams and all. But by fall, when their money's gone and winter's coming on and their crops haven't matured . . . well, you know what'll happen."

I nodded. The same thought had been in my mind. Time and climate in the end would whip them for us, but I respected John Mathers even if he was a wild-eyed dreamer. And his daughter Nela. I wished I could save them from the misery which was bound to lie ahead for them.

I got up. "I'm not going to fight a war by myself, if that's what you're afraid of."

"No, I wasn't afraid of that, but I have been worried that you wouldn't be in position to take charge when the time came." She rose and came to me. "Will, the nearest law officer is in Canon City. As long as there were just a few of us living here, it didn't make any difference, but it does now. When the colony breaks up, there may be stealing and killing, and it's hard to tell what else. What you've got to do is to go to Canon City and get yourself appointed deputy. You see what that will do for you?"

I thought about it a moment, not at all sure I could get a deputy's badge. A man like John Mathers represented fifty votes, a fact that would not be overlooked by the Canon City sheriff as individual settlers had been ignored in the past. I knew, too, that if I used force in the valley I might wind up an outlaw, even if I was a deputy to start with.

"Yeah, I see," I said. "It might do several things for me."

"Well?" Kathy asked.

"I'll think it over," I said, and left the house.

That night Red Thurston rode in, calling out to me, "Hear you need a good man."

"That we do," I said. "What happened? I thought Alec wasn't going to let you go for a few days?"

"You ain't heard?" he asked, his lips curling in disgust. When I shook my head, he said, "Alec sold out to John Mathers."

Chapter Fifteen

RED THURSTON WAS A GOOD COWHAND, A LONG-BONED, long-muscled man just a month younger than I was, with hair as fiery as a sunset over the Sangre de Cristo range. He seemed pleased that I had asked Dodson for him. Joe Pardee had given the Box P a reputation that could not be destroyed overnight.

The only effort that had been made to keep Mathers and the colonists out of the valley was ours. According to Red, our failure was blamed on Sarah rather than on me. On Alec Dodson, too, because he was president of the association and had refused to take any responsibility.

"You can't go on working for a man you don't look up to," Red said one night, "and I'm damned if anybody looks up to Alec Dodson. Not even his wife."

Because we were busy with spring roundup until the last of May, I didn't hear much of the valley news for several weeks. I didn't want to. Our position was clear, and I think everyone in the valley knew what it was. We would defend Box P range. Nothing more.

Alec Dodson loaded his personal possessions into a wagon and left the valley with his wife. That much I did hear. When I told Red, he said scornfully: "Scared out. Sold Anchor for half what it was worth." I didn't know whether this was true or not, but Dodson was gone, and so were all of his men except Red.

I put up a sign east of Carlton: BOX P RANGE. NO ADMITTANCE EXCEPT ON BUSINESS. TRESPASSING WILL BE DEALT WITH PROMPTLY. I sent a letter to Mathers, just in case he didn't know what to expect from us, saying in part, "We will not make any trouble for you if you stay on your side of the valley, but I want to make it clear that we will not surrender one blade of Box P grass to any of your people."

That was the body of the letter, and it said all I wanted to say. I did not show it to Sarah. She honestly believed, I thought, that John Mathers would and could keep his word about not letting his people settle on our range, but I didn't. None of the valley people did, as far as I knew. Certainly Irv Costello and Eric Brahms didn't.

Costello owned Skull, and Brahms the Rafter A, spreads about the size of the Box P that lay to the south of us and of Anchor. The two men rode in late on a Sunday afternoon during the last of May, sour-faced and jumpy.

"We're calling a meeting of the ranchers for tonight in the schoolhouse," Costello said. "We're going to organize again."

"With Anchor?" I asked.

Costello swore. "No. You heard who's going to rod Anchor?" I shook my head. He said, "Merle Turner."

I wasn't surprised. Mathers had said he trusted Turner. I looked at Red Thurston. He said, "Might as well turn a wolf loose in the valley."

Costello nodded. "That's a fact. I heard he was responsible for Mathers coming here. He ain't one to forget a grudge."

I didn't believe Mathers knew Turner's background or reason for returning to the valley, but whether he did or not, this looked like trouble. As foreman of Anchor, Turner was in a position of authority, and that made him far more dangerous than if he were simply another man among fifty colonists. Though I hadn't heard anything about Gene Dillingham since he'd left the Box P, except that he was still in the valley, I still believed that sooner or later he'd get together with Turner.

Costello and Brahms were watching me closely. Brahms said, "We want you at the meeting tonight."

I shook my head. "Not me."

"Why?" Costello demanded.

"We had a chance to work together," I said. "I talked to every cowman in the valley at least once during the winter, and I was after Dodson a dozen times to do something, but he wouldn't. None of you boys would, either. Now it's too late. We'd better figure out a way to live with them."

"We haven't lost our chance," Costello said. "Mathers won't bother us if he knows we're sticking together."

I thought of Sarah and of what she would say. I shook my head. "Count me out."

"That your last word?" Brahms asked.

"That's it," I said.

"You'll regret this," Costello replied, "the day they pull down your sign and roll across the line onto your grass."

"The day they do," I said, "they're in trouble."

"Three of you," Brahms answered, "and fifty of them."

"That's right," I said. "They're still in trouble."

Costello gripped his saddle horn and leaned forward. "Listen to me, Beeson. So far the damned colonists haven't bothered us or you, but they will. There was a time when the Box P stood for something. What you make it stand for today is important to the south-end ranchers, like Curly's dad. That's why you've got to be there."

"No."

"This you or the Pardee woman talking?" Costello demanded.

"*Mrs.* Pardee," I said. "You say that again, and I'll pull you out of the saddle and beat hell out of you."

"Don't try." Costello's hand dropped to gun butt. "There's something damned queer about this whole deal. Makes a man wonder if there's something between Mrs. Pardee and Mathers."

"Get out of here, Irv," I said thickly. "Get out of here before I do something I'll be sorry for."

They sat their saddles for a long moment, staring at me, sullen and red-faced, then Costello said, "Don't ever ask us for help, Beeson." They wheeled their horses and left on the gallop. I walked away from Curly and Red, not wanting to talk to them or anyone. Costello had put into words a fear that had been in my mind for a long time.

Could there actually be something between Sarah and Mathers? He was handsome, idealistic, earnest. Sure, it was possible. She could see virtues in John Mathers she had never found in Joe Pardee.

I found her sitting on the porch, a red shawl wrapped around her shoulders, for it was a chilly evening. She said: "I'm glad you're here, Will. Even on Sunday I don't get a chance to talk to you very much."

"We've been busy," I said, and rolled a smoke.

"I know."

We were silent until I lighted the cigarette, then I said, "Costello and Brahms were here."

"I saw them. They left in a huff, didn't they?"

"Yeah, they were huffy, all right," I replied. "They're trying to get organized again. They wanted me to come to a meeting tonight."

"You're not going?"

"No."

She sighed. "I'm glad, Will." She lifted her face to look at me, and I saw the softness of her expression, a deep hunger for something she had never known. "John Mathers was here twice to see me last week."

Resentment stirred in me. "So the enemy comes visiting."

"But he isn't our enemy, Will. There's room for them and us in the valley. Some of them will fail and go away. John knows that. They've lost their lawyer already. But others will stay and succeed, and there's no reason in God's world that we should fight them."

I asked, "You like Mathers, don't you?"

"Yes, I like him," she said, "but there's more to it than that. We should have culture and good will in the valley. Friendship and neighborliness. The opposite to all we had when Joe ran everything, and to what Irv Costello and Eric Brahms are trying to bring back."

"Why don't you marry Ben Sawhill?" I asked quickly. "He's a fine man."

"Ah, he *is* a fine man," she said softly, "but I'll never

marry again unless I know I love the man, love him so much I would give up everything for him. That's the only real test, Will.''

"I suppose," I said.

"Besides," she added, "I'll never saddle a man with a body bound to a wheel chair."

She does love Mathers, I thought. Perhaps it would be the force that in time would make her walk again. And it might be the force that would make her give up the Box P.

I said, "Good night, Sarah," and walked away.

Tomorrow I would go to Canon City and get the star, if I could. I'd be the law in Easter Valley. If I had to put John Mathers in jail, I'd do it.

Chapter Sixteen

I REACHED CANON CITY IN LATE AFTERNOON, LEFT MY HORSE in a livery stable, and went directly to Ben Sawhill's office. He was just locking up as I climbed the stairs. He seemed genuinely pleased to see me when he turned from the door.

He held out his hand. "What brings you to town, Will?"

"I need some advice," I said. "Not legal advice. Just that of a friend." I added, "At least, you're Sarah's friend."

"Yours too, Will." He got his pipe out and filled it, frowning. "I'll give you all the advice you want, but if it's got anything to do with Sarah it won't be worth a damn." He tamped the tobacco into the bowl of his pipe. "You know I asked her to marry me at Christmas and she turned me down."

"I guessed that was what happened," I said.

"I'm still in love with her." He fished a match out of his vest. "I always will be. Like the faithful dog who gets kicked off the porch."

I watched him as he lighted his pipe. He had tried to say it lightly, but it hadn't come off.

I waited until he had his pipe going, then I said, "Let's get supper at the hotel."

"Suits me," he said. "I didn't get out for dinner. I've got a case coming up tomorrow and I've had my nose in lawbooks all day."

We turned down the stairs and angled across the street to the hotel. We didn't talk until we gave our orders, then he leaned back in his chair, nodded at me, and said, "Let's have it."

Because we were alone in one corner of the room, there was no danger we would be overheard. He had not been in the valley since Easter. When I asked him if he'd heard what was going on, he shook his head.

"No. Just that there was some shooting, but it didn't stop Mathers."

I started in, back early in the winter, and even before that, when Sarah had given me half the ranch and told me she was the senior partner. The waitress brought oyster soup, and I dumped a handful of crackers into it and went on talking. He listened while he ate. When the girl brought our steaks and side dishes, my soup had not been touched.

"Leave his soup, Lizzie," Sawhill said.

"Ain't it good?" she asked belligerently.

"Sure. My friend here hasn't got unwound yet."

"Cowboys," she said, and sniffed, and stalked across the dining room to the kitchen.

"Doesn't she like cowboys?" I asked.

Sawhill grinned. "She's been engaged to three of them, but her loop keeps slipping off." He picked up his fork and looked at me. "That the story?"

"That's it," I said, and began to eat.

"What do you want advice about?"

I felt foolish. "I don't know," I said. "I mean, what's done is done and we can't back up. Since you're Sarah's lawyer, I figured you ought to know what's going on." I put my spoon down. "Aw, hell, Ben, it's simple enough. I guess I want you to tell me I did the right thing."

"You did the only thing you could," he said.

"Well, what should I do now?" I asked. "Sometimes I think I'll go crazy, trying not to hurt Sarah and still doing what I think I've got to do."

He nodded. "Let me think it over."

After we finished eating and stepped into the street, he said: "Will, if you get into a shooting scrape trying to keep the colonists off Box P range, you can make an outlaw out of yourself mighty fast. Thought about that?"

"Yes, I have." I was reminded of Kathy's suggestion, and asked, "You know the sheriff?"

"Sure I know him. I've been a member of his posse twice."

"Got any influence with him?"

"A little, I guess. Why?"

"We need a law man in the valley. I sure don't want it to be one of the settlers, so I figured you might talk the sheriff into appointing me."

"You're thinking off the top of your head," Sawhill said. "I can get the sheriff to give you the star, but you'd better be damned sure you want it. Are you?"

"Well, I thought I was."

"Take a good look first," he said. We turned down a side street, walking slowly, Sawhill pulling hard on his pipe. "You had no legal right to put that No Trespassing sign where it is. You own the quarter-section where the house and other buildings and corrals are. It goes across the creek and includes most of your hay meadows. That's all. If some of Mathers' bunch settle on what you claim is Box P range, the law is on their side. If you attack them, you're breaking the law. On the other hand, if you go back toting a star you're obligated to take the settlers' side if they settle on your range."

We walked in silence for a long time. I could see nothing wrong with his reasoning. "I guess I don't want the star," I said finally. "I might just as well have stayed home."

"No, I'm glad I know all you've told me," he said. "Take Merle Turner. I hadn't heard he was back. He got out of the country barely ahead of a murder indictment. The trouble now is that the witnesses are dead or gone except Art Delaney, and I doubt if he'd testify."

"No, I don't figure he would," I said.

"Another thing," Sawhill said somberly. "I can understand Sarah's feelings about John Mathers. He comes from a different world. Like she said, he stands for culture and good will. Could be she's in love with him."

"She says she'll never saddle a man with a body bound to a wheel chair."

"Maybe she won't be bound to a wheel chair all her life.

Her doctor says there's no physical reason she can't walk. She will someday if she wants to bad enough."

"Hogwash," I said. "Think she likes that wheel chair?"

"No, she doesn't like it," Sawhill said. "The trouble is, she doesn't think she can walk and the doctor hasn't been able to make her believe she can. It's got something to do with the shock when Pardee made her ride that horse and she got thrown."

"You know about that?"

"She told me at Christmas, and I had another talk with Doc when I got back. He can't explain it, but he says he's read about cases like hers."

I said gloomily, "Looks to me like I'll be in jail by fall."

"You'd better take a good long look," he said. "Personally, I'm on your side, not Sarah's. If she has her way, she'll end up by losing everything she's got. I hated Joe Pardee, but he was as practical as the gun he used."

Sawhill knocked his pipe out against his heel and slipped it into his coat pocket. "Law is one thing. Practical justice in a particular situation is often entirely different. I grant that Mathers may be honest in what he's trying to do. On the other hand, you're right in saying he'll bring misery to a lot of people; and it would have saved trouble if you could have kept him out. Now then." Sawhill put a hand on my shoulder. "Don't get carried away by your beliefs, Will. Are you willing to risk going to jail to save the Box P?"

"I've backed up as far as I can," I said. "And there's the chance that Mathers will keep his word."

Sawhill dropped his hand. "You know better. I'm not one to read the future by looking at the bottom of my teacup, but I know people, and I know how much good land there is on Anchor range."

As we walked toward the hotel, doubts began nagging me. How did a man know if he was doing the right thing? I could never pursue a direct, ruthless course as Joe Pardee had, completely confident that he was right and that all of his opponents were wrong.

We stopped in front of the hotel. I said, "Let's have a drink, Ben."

"No, I've got to get back to my case." He held out his hand. "All I've got to say is, I'm glad you're rodding the Box P, not Dillingham."

"So am I," I said, and shook hands.

"Where is Dillingham?"

"In the valley somewhere. At least, I haven't heard of his leaving."

"Watch your back," Sawhill said, and turning, crossed the street to his office.

I did not return to the Box P until the next evening. Sarah was gone. When I asked Maria, she said laconically, "She take ride with Dogbone." Curly and Red Thurston rode in a few minutes later, but they had been gone all day and didn't know where she was. I walked around the yard, smoking and wondering if I should start looking for them.

Just as Maria beat the triangle for supper, I saw the buggy coming up the road. I brought Sarah's wheel chair from the house and waited beside it under the cottonwoods.

When the buggy stopped, I lifted Sarah from the seat and placed her in the chair. Dogbone drove on to the corral. Sarah knew where I had been, but she didn't ask what I had done or if I had seen Ben Sawhill.

"I've been to see John Mathers," she said as if there was nothing unusual about such a visit. "They're making wonderful progress, Will. They have a few cabins up and some land plowed."

My blood began to pound in my head. I wanted to scold her, to say we were going to have a hard enough time without her making it harder. But she was the senior partner. I had no business telling her where she could go and whom she could see.

"Will." Sarah turned her head to look at me. "Nela invited both of us for Sunday dinner, but she said she didn't think you'd come because you're afraid of her."

"So she thinks I'm afraid of her," I said hotly. "Well, I'll show her. I'll go."

I spent the next week wondering why I had fallen into as simple a trap as that. But maybe I hadn't fallen. Maybe I just wanted an excuse to see her again.

Chapter Seventeen

On Sunday we took the two-seated rig, Maria riding in the back, Sarah in front with me. We'd had a heavy rain early in the week, and there still were pools of muddy water in low places and along the sides of the road. After the rain the weather had turned warm, unusually so for early June, and so it was now, with a bright sun in the sky that held only a few cottony clouds.

Sarah wore no wrap except a light coat which she laid across her knees. Her bonnet was a small blue one, very pert and attractive. If she was setting out to make John Mathers notice her, she was going about it the right way.

The thought occurred to me that I was putting too much emphasis on Sarah's interest in Mathers. She always dressed neatly, for she was a genius with thread and needle. I couldn't imagine anyone who would have enjoyed sewing for a baby more than Sarah.

If Sarah had had a baby, her life might have been entirely different. Maybe she would have focused her attention on her home instead of on the valley and the life of fear that Joe Pardee had forced upon it.

As we rode, both of us silent, it seemed to me that, paradoxically, I both loved and hated Sarah. I considered it as we passed Kathy Morgan's place, Sarah staring straight ahead; we clattered across the bridge, the brawling creek rushing under it, and went on through Carlton, a ghost town on Sunday morning, and then started up the West Fork, passing one covered wagon after another.

After I thought about it awhile, the business of loving and hating Sarah began to make sense. I loved her because of all the things she had done for me, and because she loved me, and I was sure she did. I loved her for the goodness and gentleness that were so much a part of her. But I hated her because I was afraid of what she would do to me in the future, and to the Box P. Then I thought of John Mathers. He was the one I should hate, I thought, because he had brought all of this on us.

I was not in a pleasant mood when we reached the settlement that the colonists called Amity. This was their town; they had their own store, and they were going to petition for a post office. As far as they were concerned, Carlton might as well not have existed. Art Delaney wouldn't get a nickel's worth of trade from these people he had welcomed.

We had passed several patches of turned sod, brown where it should have been green. The farmers were fighting against time in an effort to get a crop in the fall. Now, as I saw the amount of building that had been done in the few weeks the colonists had been here, I wondered if the carpenters outnumbered the farmers.

The largest building was on the right side of the road. This, I learned, was the store managed by Al Romig. There was a partition at one end which set off a small room that was Mathers' office. Across the road was a slightly smaller building with a sign that said COMMUNITY CENTER. Here, Sarah told me, they held Sunday service, business meetings, and Saturday-night dances, and in the winter it would be the schoolhouse.

I judged that at least twenty of the fifty families lived in the settlement. Half a dozen cabins had been built farther up the road, and scattered among them were ten or fifteen tents. What had been done so far was impressive, but it was the long haul that counted, not the short one.

A crowd was waiting for us when we stopped. John Mathers stepped forward, calling to a man to take the team. After Mathers shook hands with me, I lifted Sarah from the rig, carried her inside, and set her down in a rocking chair. After that we had to shake hands with everyone, even the children, who stared at my gun with solemn eyes.

The adults had no way of knowing that Gene Dillingham's presence in the valley forced me to carry a gun to church, and I didn't explain. Though I didn't actually know Dillingham was here, I was sure he wouldn't leave until he'd settled his score with me.

The pews were unplaned planks laid across blocks of wood, and the pulpit was a narrow platform about two feet high. Mathers took his place behind an up-ended crate, opened the service with a prayer and a hymn, and then welcomed Sarah and Maria and me, saying we were the first of the valley residents to attend one of their functions. He hoped that we would not be the last and that we would feel welcome to come again. Another hymn and a scripture reading were followed by a sermon, a short one because the seats had become uncomfortable by the time he started.

I studied Mathers' people as he preached. They didn't look at all like the professional wandering homeseekers we had seen repeatedly in the valley, the kind of men, for instance, who would hire Al Beam to shoot Joe Pardee.

They were all ages, some too old to be tackling the job they had set out to do. Some had been toughened by weeks of hard work they had put in since they had reached the valley, but others looked as if they would never adapt themselves to their new life.

I wanted to hate these people. They had no business coming here in the first place. They had disrupted a way of life that had suited me, a good life that was meant to be lived in this particular valley. Because they threatened our future, Sarah's and mine, at least, I had come prepared to hate them; but I honestly could not, now that I sat here and looked at them.

If there was one characteristic common to all of them, it was sincerity. I had felt this quality in Mathers from the first time I had met him last fall, and I sensed it in his sermon. There was none of the hellfire-and-brimstone preaching that I was accustomed to hearing once a month in the little church in Carlton. Instead, he talked about faith, emphasizing how

Abraham had left his home and gone to a strange land and had made a new life for himself just as they were doing in Easter Valley.

John Mathers couldn't have been more wrong if he'd had two left feet, and everyone who had come with him was wrong; but after he dismissed us with a prayer and all of us filed out quietly and solemnly, I could not find it in me to blame them for being here. They'd try, and the failure which would eventually be their destiny would not be their fault.

Nela came to us, saying she would run over to their cabin and get dinner started. Sarah sent Maria to help her. Several lingered to talk. Al Romig was one. Len Scott, the colony's secretary, was another. He was a small, intense man who crackled with enthusiasm and confidence. His wife was a bosomy woman who stood a full head taller than Scott. She hung on every word he said as if he had a direct pipeline to the Lord. They all seemed good people, and how can you hate good people?

After the last one left with a hope we would come again, I picked Sarah up and carried her to Mathers' cabin across the road and upstream from the store and office building. Mathers brought the rocking chair, and after we had made her comfortable she said: "John, I hate being a burden like this. Someday I won't be. I'm going to walk. You'll see."

Mathers looked at her, his eyes locked with hers. He said confidently: "You will, Sarah. You have the faith that it takes."

I went outside and rolled a cigarette, sick with a cold, aching pain far down inside me. I told myself they had no right to be in love.

Presently Mathers joined me. He said, "A man is always underfoot when women are preparing a meal."

I nodded and went on smoking. Then he said, his voice low so that Sarah could not hear: "Beeson, I know you consider us your enemy. Does it have to be that way?"

"I don't see how it can be any other way."

He was silent for a time. From somewhere on the other side of the creek a meadow lark's sweet song came to us. Overhead a hawk sailed gracefully through the air. All was peaceful and quiet, with now and then the voice of a child calling to another from one of the tents or cabins. Smoke rose from a dozen cook fires as women prepared Sunday dinners just as Nela was doing.

Finally Mathers said softly: "This is what I have dreamed about for years: a chance to help people help themselves. If you could have seen the way they were living . . ." He looked at me and shook his head. "No, I guess it wouldn't have made any difference to you."

"Mathers," I said, "you still don't know what you've done, do you?"

"I know, but you don't." He stroked his beard as he said: "Your letter was entirely unnecessary. I have told you, and I have promised Mrs. Pardee, that we will not in any way harm you or your stock or your ranch. Why do you keep harping on it?"

"Because I know what's coming," I answered. "Right now everybody is happy, but in the long run you'll find out you've brought nothing but misery to a lot of people."

He shook his head, his gentle face filled with pity. "Beeson, I bought Dodson's ranch, spending money I could ill afford to spend, but I bought it because I wanted to prevent bloodshed."

I motioned toward the creek bottom. "How much land are you giving your farmers?"

"It varies," he said. "Up on the bench some have eighty acres, or as much as a hundred. On the creek, where we can put water on the land and where it's good deep soil, they have forty acres."

"There's your answer, Mathers," I said. "Next fall you'll see. Because your farmers will find out they're not in Missouri where they could raise good crops, they'll look across the valley at Box P range and they'll say to themselves that they need more land and that it's waiting for them over there. Not forty acres, Mathers, but a whole quarter-section that won't cost them a penny. They'll come and I'll be waiting, and what do you think will happen then?"

His hands fisted at the sides of his long-tailed black coat.

"You won't harm them, Beeson," he said. "Sarah won't let you."

"That's where you're wrong," I said. "Let's get another thing straight. Are you courting Sarah just to make it easy for your people to get more land?"

That hurt him. "Beeson," he said, and I felt ashamed, "I love her. I've asked her to marry me, but she won't until she can walk. Someday she will, but regardless of when that day comes I will not do a single thing to hurt her."

I said, "Maybe you won't hurt her, but some of your people will."

He looked at me again, and I sensed the worry and anxiety that was in him; but he didn't have a chance to say anything more, for just then Nela called, "Dinner's ready," and Mathers and I went into the cabin together.

Chapter Eighteen

THE MATHERS CABIN WAS FAR FROM FINISHED. A RANGE took up one corner, with the wall on the other side of the stove covered by shelves from the floor to the ceiling. Here were piled the pots and pans and dishes, and sacks of supplies. The floor was of earth, but Mathers had put shakes on the roof so they would not have the usual dirty dribble that afflicted cabins with sod roofs when it rained.

The furniture, I judged, had been brought from Missouri: a table, a few straight-backed chairs, two rocking chairs, and an oak stand with sprawling legs that were capped by ugly metal fingers clutching glass balls. On the stand was a tiny music box which I suspected belonged to Nela.

"A lot of work still to be done on the cabin," Mathers said apologetically, "but we're putting it off until winter when the weather's too bad to work outside."

"You've done wonderfully well, John," Sarah said.

"I'm satisfied," Mathers admitted, "but I do want to put up a lean-to for Nela so she'll have her own room. She's sleeping in the tent back of the cabin and I'm sleeping in the wagon. We can get along comfortably enough until cold weather, but I'd hate to spend the winter where we are."

Nela was wearing a white dress with a ruffly lace collar that gave a tone of primness to her, a deceiving touch, I thought. Now that I had an opportunity really to look at her, I took advantage of it. She tried to be lady-like, but her snub nose and square chin gave me the impression she was a tomboy at heart. Even when the conversation was serious, her gray eyes held a twinkle of laughter.

She was prettier than I had first thought. Her face had lost the peeled look and was smoothly tanned; and I liked the speed with which she put a good meal on the table. She was a city girl, but she certainly hadn't been spoiled by city living.

She caught me staring at her and winked boldly at me. I lowered my head, my face hot with embarrassment. She looked down, too, laughing silently, and I wished I had her outside alone where I could deal with her properly.

I didn't know much about women. The floozies in Canon City would steal a starving man's last dollar if they could, and all the glittering sequins they wore and the stinking perfume they doused themselves with couldn't change them.

Of course, there were a few valley girls. Curly King had a sixteen-year-old sister who wanted to get married so bad I was afraid to be seen with her. Irv Costello had an eighteen-year-old daughter who was a good cook, but her face, according to the talk in Delaney's store, had started more stampedes in Easter Valley than all other causes combined. The girls who would make good wives were picked off at once; the rest were culls that a man wouldn't want to be caught getting into bed with.

A hell of a situation, I thought. By fall Nela would be married. The colony probably had some single men who were interested in her, and I could name at least six eligible cowboys who would be camping in front of Mathers' cabin from now until one of them got her roped and tied. As far as I was concerned, I'd go after her so hard my tracks would be smoking if she hadn't been John Mathers' daughter.

Nela rose the instant we finished her three-layer cake. "Dad, will you help Maria do the dishes? I'm going to ask Mr. Beeson to take me for a ride."

"It strikes me you're a little presumptuous," Mathers said. "You don't know Mr. Beeson will take you for a ride, and asking a guest to do the dishes—"

"Of course Maria will do the dishes," Sarah broke in. "I

can dry. You won't have to help, John." She nodded at me. "Will, you go ahead."

"Sure," I said, and, getting up, whirled my chair around like a showoff. "Come on, Miss Mathers. You want a ride. You'll get one."

By the time I brought the rig to the front of the cabin, she was waiting. Clouds boiling up over the Sangre de Cristos had turned the day cool. Nela had put on her coat and a wool cap which came down over her ears. She didn't wait until I stepped down and offered her a hand. She jumped into the seat beside me, saying, "Don't get any wrong ideas in your head; I want to go to the ranch, but being subtle isn't one of my talents."

"The ranch?"

"Anchor," she said impatiently. "You heard we bought it, didn't you?"

I drove up the road, staring straight ahead. I had forgotten all about Mathers buying Anchor, but that wasn't what bothered me. It was Nela, sitting beside me, her shoulder touching mine. I had been floored by her asking me to take her for a ride. Even the boy-crazy King girl wouldn't have played the game that openly.

"You *had* heard, hadn't you?" she asked.

"Yeah, sure." I swallowed. "Look, Miss Mathers, I . . ."

"Nela," she said.

"All right, Nela. I was going to say I can't figure you out. I never intended to ask you, I mean, I . . ."

She put a stop to my floundering. "I know exactly what you mean. To you I am one of the enemy. As for me, I accepted you as a guest at our table out of deference to Mrs. Pardee. I realize that asking a man to take me for a ride is not being lady-like, but I assure you I can be lady-like when I have to. I didn't have time today. I couldn't ask Dad to take me and I couldn't go off by myself and leave everybody." Her voice had been cool and distant, but now she smiled, and added with some warmth, "I just did what I thought would work."

"Why do you have to go to the ranch?"

"Merle Turner's running it for Dad." She looked squarely

at me. "Last week Turner hired Gene Dillingham. I want to see what they're doing."

I was shocked, but only for a moment. I realized at once it was a natural alliance, with Dillingham and Turner old friends and both having practically the same grudge. I remembered that the thought had once occurred to me that Dillingham might go over to the colonists.

"If Dillingham's there," I said finally, "you'd better stay outside. Or don't you know what will happen when we meet?"

"Nothing will happen today," she said. "At least, I don't think so. Turner and Dillingham aren't ready."

"Ready for what?"

"I'm not sure. Maybe to steal everything they can. Mr. Beeson, I want to know—"

"Will."

She laughed. "All right, Will. We might as well pretend to be friends because I'm not going to give up our side and you won't give up Mrs. Pardee, so we'll see each other whether we like it or not. I started to ask why you're so sure we'll fail. Don't give me the standard arguments. I know all of them, and they aren't good enough."

"What are the standard arguments?"

"You know them if anyone does," she answered tartly. "This is cattle country. Short growing season. Crops won't mature."

"All facts," I said.

"Maybe, but there's more to it than that, isn't there? I mean, with you. You're afraid, so you'll fight and perhaps die because you're afraid."

"I'm not afraid." Then I realized what she had said was true. "Well, maybe I am. I'm afraid your dad will make Sarah hate me. I'm afraid your people will move in on us regardless of what your dad can do. I'm afraid they'll destroy the valley by plowing up fields that should be left in grass. Is that enough things to be afraid of?"

"Yes," she said, "and I'm afraid, too. I love my father. That's why I left a comfortable home to come with him. He was doing well. He owned a hardware store that was giving him a good living, but he got this harebrained scheme and he just had to come. I know he'll fail as well as you know it, but for different reasons.''

I turned off the road and started up the steep slope that led to the Anchor buildings. I looked at her, feeling common ground between us for the first time.

"What are your reasons?" I asked.

"I know Dad," she said. "He was a good hardware man because he understood his business. But on this colony project, he thinks in terms of how he wants it to be, and he gets carried away so completely he can't see conditions as they actually are.''

"Like the climate?"

She nodded. "But it was the people I had in mind. Because he was sure everything would be just as he planned, a well rounded community, he figured out how many farmers we'd need, how many carpenters, a preacher, a doctor, and so on. Most of the money that went into the project was his, and a lot of the folks signed up because he was paying for their passage out here. I don't think they ever intended to stay with the colony.''

"I thought the people in church looked pretty solid.''

"Most of the folks you saw were farmers. They're the ones who will stay.''

"I heard you had lost your lawyer.''

"And our doctor and preacher and gunsmith and three carpenters.''

Now I understood why Mathers had preached. We drew up in front of the house, and I wrapped the lines around the brake handle and stepped down, wondering what Mathers would eventually do with Anchor. If his ignorance of the cattle business didn't break him, Merle Turner would.

Nela and I walked up the path to the house, and it seemed to me that in the short time Alec Dodson had been gone a noticeable decay had set in, little things that in time would become big things. Dodson had always been fussy about keeping everything in its exact place, but what I saw now indicated Turner didn't give a damn.

I followed Nela through the front door into the living room.

It looked like a boar's nest. Four men were playing cards, but Dillingham was not one of them. Turner was there, looking exactly as I remembered him: big head, red eyes, and fang-like teeth which were never quite hidden even when his lips were closed.

"Howdy, Nela," Turner said, and went on playing.

"Merle, I want you to meet Will Beeson from the Box P," Nela said.

Turner put his cards down and rose, his red-veined eyes pinned on me. He surprised me by taking two steps toward me and holding out his hand. I gripped it and he sat down again. "Will Beeson," he murmured as if he had trouble placing me. "I remember you. Worked for Joe Pardee, didn't you?"

I nodded. "You remember me, all right."

He shrugged. "I remember Joe Pardee, too. I hear he finally got what was coming to him."

"He was shot, if that's what you mean."

He started to say something, but picked up his cards instead. Nela introduced me to the others: Hec Troy, Lew Secore, and Lin Runyan, ordinary men who would probably follow Turner in any direction he took.

"We missed you this morning in church," Nela said.

The three looked embarrassed, but Turner shrugged. "We got started on this game early this morning," he said. "You know how it is when you work hard all week."

"Dad preached," Nela said.

"That's good," Turner said. "Give me two, Lin."

Nela looked at me and nodded toward the door. "Where's Dillingham, Turner?" I asked.

"Gene? Oh, he went to town, I think."

I left with Nela, sure that Turner was lying, but if Dillingham wanted to stay under cover while I was there, I'd let it go at that. What Nela had said about them not being ready was probably right.

I helped Nela into the rig, and went around the back and climbed in beside her. She retained her composure until we were out of sight of the house. Then she began to cry. I pulled up and put an arm around her. She came to me willingly, lowering her head against my shoulder, but only for a minute; then she straightened and pushed my arm away.

"I hate weepy women, Will," she said, "but I did need your strong shoulder for a minute. Everything finally piled up on me. I didn't think Turner would be working today. I don't think he's worked since Dad sent him up there. I just had to go see what was happening. Dad spent so much money for the place, not even knowing what he was getting. Just taking Turner's word."

Because there was nothing I could say, nothing I could do, we rode in silence until we reached the cabin. She got down, said, "Thank you," and ran inside. A moment later she called from the doorway, "Sarah's ready to go home, Will," so I waited. John Mathers appeared in the doorway with Sarah in his arms; he carefully set her in the seat beside me, then kissed her and stepped back.

I said, "Goodbye," and touched the brim of my hat to Nela, who was standing just outside the cabin. She smiled and waved. We drove fifty yards in silence, then Sarah said, "Now you know about John and me."

"Yes," I said. "I knew before," and after that neither one of us felt like talking.

Chapter Nineteen

WE DID NOT GO BACK TO THE COLONISTS' SETTLEMENT OR to Mathers' place. Sarah said it was too hard on her. She'd rather stay at home where she was familiar with everything and had her wheel chair. Instead, Mathers and Nela came to the Box P for Sunday dinners. As soon as the meals were finished, Nela and I always took a walk, or I'd saddle up a couple of horses and we'd go for a ride.

I was not aware of it at first, but it wasn't long before I knew I was in love with her. I wasn't sure just how she felt, and I was afraid to find out. Even if she did love me, there was no future for us so far as I could tell.

So I lived for each Sunday, trying not to think about the tomorrow that was always in Mathers' mind. Every afternoon with Nela was like a too sweet dream. When they drove away near sundown, I would stand under the cottonwoods watching until I couldn't see the rig, and every time I wondered if this was the last Sunday afternoon we would have together.

Sarah kept telling me everything was going fine with the colony. Crops were looking good. More cabins were being built. Anchor steers were getting fat on the lush grass in the foothills of the Sangre de Cristos. All this was true as far as it went. Nela told me how it really was, with more and more discontent among the colonists who were finding that building new homes in the wilderness was quite different from the idyllic concept of life in Easter Valley that John Mathers had given them.

"And now Dad's broke," she said bitterly. "Just the farmers are left, and they'll stay."

She had said that before, and I'm sure she believed it. I did too, if they had enough land. That, as I had known all along, was the crux of the whole thing. It was only a question of time until they spilled out on Brahms's and Costello's grass, and on the Box P's.

I mentioned this again to Mathers when we were alone before dinner one Sunday in July. He had, as always, a happy solution. "Water is lifeblood out here," he said in his pontifical way. "We have to hold the spring runoff, so we'll build a dam somewhere above the valley. That way we'll be able to put water on the bench land above the creek. There's plenty of that, Will." Then he assumed an attitude of righteous indignation. "I've told you repeatedly and I'll tell you again: there will be no trouble."

All I could do was to sit there and count to ten thousand in the hope that I could control my temper. John Mathers may have been, as Nela said, a good hardware merchant, but he wasn't the right man to head a colony of settlers.

Nela had told me the colony's treasury was almost depleted, and the dam Mathers was talking about required both labor and money for materials and engineers' service. But I didn't try to tell Mathers that. I knew I couldn't tell him anything.

So we lived through much of the summer, waiting for the bubble to break. Then, one evening in August, with purple twilight steadily deepening in the valley, I crossed the front porch of the house and stepped through the doorway. I stopped, flat-footed, unable to breathe. Sarah was on her feet, a full two steps in front of her wheel chair. I hadn't seen her stand upright since her accident.

I stood there staring at her, and she looked back at me. The light inside the house was so dim I could not make out the expression on her face, but it must, I thought, be one of sheer ecstasy because she was finally demonstrating what she had long ago said she could do.

Suddenly she cried, "Will, look! I can walk! I told you I

would." She took two more steps toward me, slow, hesitant steps, then toppled headlong to the floor.

I ran to her and picked her up. "I'm all right, Will," she whispered. "I'm all right." I would have taken her to her bed but she wouldn't let me. "Put me on the couch," she said. "I'm not hurt, I tell you."

I obeyed, and then I wanted to call María, but she wouldn't let me do that, either. "Just let me rest here a few minutes," she said, "and then put me in the chair. I've been doing two steps forward and two back. I wanted to surprise you, but I didn't hear you come in, and when I saw you I got excited and thought I could walk to you. I should have known better. I suppose it will be months before I can walk across the room, but I *am* improving, Will."

I pulled up a chair and sat down beside the couch. She reached out and took my hand and squeezed it, whispering, "Will, you didn't believe me, did you?"

"I do now," I said.

I leaned forward until I was close enough to see the beads of sweat on her forehead, the expression of agony on her face. It must have been painful for her to stand up, let alone walk. Then her fall . . .

"Sarah," I said, "do you love Mathers so much that you've got to walk for him?"

"Maybe it isn't just him," she said. "I've been a drag on you for a long time. Maybe I want to walk for your sake, Will. Have you thought of that?"

"No. You haven't been a drag on me. I thought it was Mathers—" I stopped, completely confused by what she had said, and added lamely, "It just doesn't seem right to be torturing yourself."

"I've got to, Will." She still held my hand, and her face seemed devoid of expression in the fading twilight. "Will, aren't you getting too interested in Nela?"

My heart started to pound. This was the first time Sarah had mentioned it. She didn't sound at all pleased.

"We always clear out after dinner so you and Mathers can visit," I said.

"That's very thoughtful of you," she said, quite coolly,

"but I had the impression you were enjoying each other's company. I don't want you to be hurt, Will. You're so young, and you've never been in love. If you aren't careful, it can destroy you."

I sat there in silence, not moving, Sarah still holding my hand. I didn't know what to say, but I realized that if anyone knew what love could do to a person, it was Sarah.

"You're not like me," she went on. "The ranch isn't first with me. It is with you. But remember this. John can't change, and Nela is his daughter. Forget her, Will. You've got to forget her. Don't you see what will happen to both of you if you don't?"

I drew my hand from hers and stood up. What she had said didn't make sense. If John Mathers was good for her, then Nela must be good for me. Of course, I knew Nela much better than Sarah did, and one of the first things I had learned was that Nela was almost as impatient with her father as I was.

I rolled a cigarette, taking my time, and lighted it. Good Lord, I thought, *Sarah is jealous of Nela.* Because of me, Will Beeson, who was almost a son to her. At least, she was the nearest thing to a mother I had ever known.

It was crazy. I was sixteen when I had come here, Sarah twenty-eight. Now I was twenty-four, and she was thirty-six, and in love with John Mathers. And yet, now that I thought about it, I could remember so many things she had done for me, things I had no right to expect, and I remembered how often she had held my hand just as she had now.

I flipped my cigarette into the yard and walked back to the couch. I said, "Sarah, how much does the Box P mean to you?"

She had been lying down, her head against one arm of the couch, but now she sat up, moving with more agility than usual, bracing herself with her hands on both sides of her. "Will, I'm glad you've given me a chance to tell you. I hate it. Joe never belonged to me. He was a bigamist. He was married to the ranch before he married me. I fought the Box P from the day we were married, and I always lost. It was first with him and I was second. Not just the Box P but the whole valley. And now it's the same with you."

"It's not the valley with me," I said.

"The ranch, then. It's put you out of my reach. You're like a stream moving away from me all the time. It's not that important."

"It's put money in the bank for you," I said. "It'll put some more there after roundup."

"I still hate it," she said vehemently.

"Then don't live here. You'll be marrying Mathers before long. Until then you can live in Canon City. I'll buy your half. I'll give you my note, or maybe I can borrow enough."

She didn't answer for a long time. Darkness was complete now. I stood close to her, her shape vague in the starshine that came through the windows and open door. Then she said, "Light a lamp, Will."

I obeyed, and when I turned to her she held her arms up to me. "Put me back into the chair," she said. I picked her up and carried her to the chair and set her down. She clung to me more than she needed to; her hands did not release me as soon as they could have. She said: "Thank you, Will, but I won't sell out now. I wouldn't put that burden upon you. I don't hate the Box P so much I can't live on it."

I said, "Good night, Sarah," and left the room.

Dogbone was already in bed, and Curly and Red Thurston were pulling off their boots when I went into the bunkhouse. Red said: "I forgot to tell you, Will. I ran into Irv Costello today when I was taking salt up to Deadman's Flat. He said Brahms has lost several steers. He figures the colonists are living off his beef, and he's sent for the sheriff."

"It's his trouble," I said.

"Maybe ours," Curly said, "if them plow pushers get hungry enough."

I didn't argue. Curly might be right, but this wasn't the night for me to worry about it. I went to bed, and Red blew out the lamp; but it was a long, long time after that before the first pale light of dawn touched the eastern windows. I hadn't slept at all, but I had reached a decision. If Nela Mathers would have me, I'd marry her right away.

Chapter Twenty

THE SHERIFF CAME FROM CANON CITY, LOOKED AROUND, asked some questions, and rode away without making any arrests, much to Eric Brahms's disgust. I saw Irv Costello in Delaney's store that Saturday.

"Them bastards will go right on eating our beef," he said bitterly. "If I catch one of 'em at it, I'll hang him. By God, I will!"

But it was none of my business and, in my opinion, none of Costello's. I had more pressing problems. The next Sunday, which was the last one in August, was the breaking point as far as I was concerned.

Some decisions are relatively easy ones to make. Whether to hang a settler for stealing Brahms's cattle was one. To fight or not to fight was another, or should be. Whether to ask a woman to marry you is a third, if you love her as I loved Nela. The fact that John Mathers was her father did add complications, but I could leave that up to Nela.

The problem that kept me awake night after night was what to do about Sarah. It was a decision I couldn't make because suddenly I woke up to the fact that I didn't understand her.

I had looked upon Sarah as an angel with a shattered body. After Joe's death I blamed him for all the trouble they'd had, for making Sarah a cripple, for forcing a rule of fear upon the valley which Sarah deplored.

Looking back over the past year, I realized that my attitude toward Joe had been changed by what Sarah had said, slowly and insidiously, but changed just the same. Now I habitually thought of Joe as Sarah wanted me to think of him.

I felt as if I had been forcibly shaken awake while in the middle of a beautiful dream. Two things had done so. I had seen Sarah standing on her feet as erect as anyone and I had seen her take two steps. And I had heard her say I was becoming too fond of of Nela, that I must forget her, when, by all standards of common sense, she should have been happy because I was fond of Nela, who would be her step-daughter.

But it was obvious that she didn't want me to marry Nela. If I did, I wouldn't be able to bring her to the Box P as my wife. Was I, then, to walk off and leave half a ranch I owned?

Though I couldn't answer that question, I made up my mind to marry Nela, then settle the other questions later. I was afraid that Sarah would find some way or other to separate me from Nela.

As we ate Sunday dinner, we were all tense, except Mathers, who rattled on in his usual enthusiastic way, and with his usual fine choice of words. Nela must have realized something was wrong. She was silent throughout the meal. So was Sarah, but her gaze was on me constantly, a frown marring her usually sweet face.

The instant we were done eating, I rose. Apparently Nela sensed what was in my mind, for she pushed her chair back and got up, saying: "Excuse me, Mrs. Pardee. We're going for a walk."

Sarah opened her mouth to speak, but closed it without saying a word; she motioned as if to call me to her, but I pretended I didn't see it and went outside. Mathers had leaned back in his chair and filled his pipe, unperturbed and plainly unaware of the undercurrents of emotions that were tugging at the three of us.

Once outside, I walked fast, Nela running to keep up. She grabbed my arm, panting, "What's wrong, Will?"

I slowed down. "I'll tell you in a minute."

When we reached the creek, we sat down behind a screen of willows beside a long pool that was deep enough for swimming. For some reason the irrelevant thought struck me that the biggest trout Sarah had ever caught out of the East Fork had come from this pool.

"Lie down and be comfortable," I said. "I'm going to talk for a long time—about myself."

She laughed and lay on her back, her skirt pulled up far enough to expose her ankles. I stared at them, then at the firm swell of her breasts under her blouse, at her mouth with the smile still lingering in the corners, and at the dimples not more than an inch from the ends of her lips. Finally my gaze met her gray eyes.

She sat up, suddenly concerned. "Will, I never saw you look at me like that before."

I picked up a rock, tossed it into the water, and watched the circles ripple out until they died against the bank. "We've been together every Sunday lately, but you don't know much about me. It's time you did."

She dropped back to the ground, tiny patches of sunlight that slipped through the willow leaves falling on her. "I know enough, Will. I found out all I needed to know the day you had dinner with us."

"You're going to hear the rest of it," I said. "If you get bored, you can go to sleep."

"I won't go to sleep," she said softly.

"I don't remember my mother," I said. "She died when I was a baby. My father raised me until I was twelve. He taught me to read and write and spell, and figure a little, but he was a boomer, always on the move. When I was twelve he got it into his head he had to see the elephant, so we headed for Santa Fe.

"Comanches caught us when we were crossing the Jornada del Muerto, and he was killed. I went on with the wagon train. Everybody was sorry for me, but nobody wanted me except an old man who whipped me the first day he had me. When we got to Santa Fe I ran away. After that I lived the best I could, ducking and dodging and stealing sometimes. Doing any odd jobs I could. I drifted north to Cimarron, then Trinidad, and finally saved enough to buy a horse and saddle."

I stopped. It wasn't easy, telling this to the girl I hoped to marry, but I had to. It was a complex thing, tied up with my feeling for Sarah, my loyalty to the Box P, and the memory of Joe Pardee. For some reason I had made up my mind she must know most everything about me before I asked her to marry me.

"I had four years of that," I said. "The Trinidad sheriff claimed I was the orneriest kid he had ever seen. Maybe I was. I might have turned outlaw right then. I think I would have if I hadn't showed up here. Anyhow, I drifted north, asking at ranches for a job and maybe getting a little work and a meal now and then. I stopped at the King place, but I saw they were about as hungry as I was. I tried Costello's, and he kicked me off his ranch. When I got here, Sarah was fishing in this pool."

I rolled a cigarette, realizing I was breathing hard because I was reliving that moment as I had not lived it for years. I held the unlit cigarette and looked at it.

"Sarah stared at me as if I was a scarecrow. I was sixteen, dirty, riding an old nag of a mare and forking a beat-up saddle, wearing clothes that weren't fit for a ragbag, and I suppose my bones practically stuck out through my skin. I asked her for a job, and she said first I was going to take a bath. She said to strip off and jump into the creek and she'd fetch me some decent clothes. She picked up her pole and string of trout and started for the house."

Nela was sitting up, looking at me, her lips parted. I took time to light the cigarette, and she said, "Go on."

"Well, I did what she said. She got back with the clothes before I figured she would. I was in the creek, stark naked, but that didn't bother her. She said she couldn't find any boots that would fit, but the rest of the things would do. I'll never forget trying to hide down there in the water while Sarah laid the clothes she'd brought on the bank. She looked at me as unconcerned as if I was a girl and told me to get out and dress, that I had a job. I did, and she walked to the house with me. Later that day Joe took me to Delaney's store and bought me more clothes and boots that fitted."

I stopped again and pulled on the cigarette. I was remembering a lot of things: how Sarah looked before her hair turned white, straight-backed and proud and very beautiful, and how tolerant Joe was about everything she asked for. They hadn't been married long then; if she had wanted the moon he'd have done his best to put a loop on it and drag it out of the sky for her.

"Well?" Nela prompted.

"That's about all," I said, "except that for a couple of years or more I was chore boy. When Dogbone showed up, I started riding for Joe, and Dogbone took my place."

I threw my cigarette away and watched it float downstream. There was so much more I couldn't tell her: how Sarah and Joe had drifted apart, and about him going to Kathy Morgan, and Sarah's accident and her hair turning white. I'd told enough. Nela knew I'd been wild and in trouble with the law, and she knew how much I owed to Sarah. That was the part I thought she ought to know.

I said, "I guess this is about as unromantic a proposal as a man ever made, but what I started to say was that I love you and I want you to marry me."

I wasn't looking at her now. I couldn't. I hurried on: "I'm not trying to make you think I'm anything great. You know how it is between me and your dad. I'm not going to back up. Not even for Sarah. I don't have any education. No schooling, I mean. Sarah used to read to me a lot. The Bible and Plato and Shakespeare and Dickens, books her father had left her, but that doesn't help me make a living. If we have to leave the Box P and you're my wife, you might starve because I don't know anything but ranch work. With what Joe left me when he was killed, and with what I've saved, I've got a little over $1,000 in the bank in Canon City. I own a horse and saddle and a gun and my clothes. That's all."

"Will." She reached out and took my hand. "Will, can't you stop talking and listen for a while? Don't you want the answer to your question?"

I did look at her then. Her face was close to mine, and I heard her whisper: "Will, I want to marry you more than anything else in the world. Today. Tomorrow. Next week. Any time you say."

I put my arms around her and kissed her, and she clung to me with passionate fierceness, giving me an unspoken promise, and when she drew back, she said: "A woman doesn't have much chance, Will. I've loved you for so long. I thought you'd never ask me."

Then the old fear began gnawing at me. I said: "It'll raise hell when we tell Sarah and your dad. Let's get married now and tell them later. Tomorrow."

Her eyes widened as she thought about it. Maybe she was afraid just as I was. There were so many things that might happen. "Will, we can't lose each other now. We just can't." Leaning back against me, with my arm around her, she said: "I've got $200 of my own. I want to put it with your money. If I don't, sooner or later Dad will get it for the colony, and I don't want him to have it. Twelve hundred dollars is enough to get started somewhere else, even, if—if we have to leave here."

Her words told me a great deal: that John Mathers was as demanding in his way as Sarah was in hers, and that even if we had to leave the Box P, we'd get along, somehow. But Sarah? My mind, alive now with memories of the bad years and of what my life might have been without Sarah, could not accept a complete break with her. But I put that out of my thoughts for the moment. My most immediate need was to marry Nela.

She turned her head, kissed me, and said, "All right, Will. Tomorrow. Where?"

"Canon City. We'll meet in the hotel." I thought how far away the town must seem to her, and I said, "How will you get there?"

"Ride. I had a horse brought down from the ranch, and Dad knows I've been aiming to go down for some clothes."

"He'll let you ride alone?"

"Of course. You're marrying a self-reliant woman, Will. I've had to be ever since Mother died six years ago."

"I'll meet you in Carlton and we'll—"

"No. I'd rather ride alone to Canon City. I don't want anyone seeing us together until it's settled. Dad might talk me out of it, and I don't want him to."

"All right, we'll meet in the hotel in Canon City as soon as you can get there."

I kissed her, holding her hard against me; and for that moment there were no problems, just Nela and me, and no sound except the breath of the wind in the willow leaves over our heads and the rush of water above the pool.

Chapter Twenty-One

ON MONDAY MORNING I LEFT AFTER BREAKFAST, THE SUN not yet up, telling María I was going to Canon City and might be gone several days. She was to inform Sarah, and say that I had given work orders to Curly and Red.

I rode hard, hoping to get to town ahead of Nela, for there were several things I wanted to do. I put my horse up, and went first to Ben Sawhill's office. When I told him what I planned, he shook my hand and slapped me on the back as he said, "I told you almost a year ago you ought to get married."

"I hadn't met Nela then," I said. "Can you get away from the office for a while?"

"Sure can," he said. "I haven't got a thing to do."

I told him to get a room for us at the hotel, and arrange for the preacher. I left then, and bought new clothes, including the first store suit I ever owned, had a shave and bath, and put on the new suit. Then, smelling of cologne, and with my suit uncomfortably tight, I went to the hotel and found Nela waiting for me in the lobby, talking to Sawhill.

When he saw me, he turned from her. "Will, you're a lucky man. My only regret is that I didn't see her before you did."

Nela, shy for the first time since I had met her, stared at the floor. "Will, I don't have any clothes, and it's too late this evening to buy them. Let's wait until morning."

"Don't wait," Sawhill said. "It's like diving into a cold pool. If you start feeling it with your big toe, you'll never make the dive."

Nela laughed uneasily, and I said, "You're in a good position to talk, Ben."

"I should know if any man does," he said. "Now listen to me, both of you, and make up your mind to do what I say. A hotel room is no place to spend your wedding night."

He put a hand on my shoulder and bowed to Nela. "I have gone to some pains this afternoon, and I'll be mighty put out if I don't get my way. I have a house that is yours as long as you're in town. My housekeeper cleaned up this morning, so it's all spic and span. Bed changed. House swept and dusted. And supper is on the stove for all of us right now." He pulled a big silver watch from a vest pocket, studied it, and announced: "In five minutes the preacher will be there. Let's start."

Nela held back. "We can't put you out like this, Mr. Sawhill. A hotel room is all we expected—"

"Miss Mathers," he said severely, "the only way you can put me out is to refuse me. I even have a bottle of champagne. If you make me drink all of it, I'll lose my practice."

"He means it," I said, and Nela reluctantly nodded agreement.

A rig was waiting outside the hotel. In less than five minutes we were in Sawhill's house, and within another ten minutes we were being married in his front room with its horsehair sofa and stuffed owl on the mantel and the framed motto on the wall, "God Bless Our Home." I looked away from it, for I was thinking of Sarah, and of Ben Sawhill who loved her, and how it would have been if she had agreed last Christmas to marry him.

So we were married, in a pleasant, friendly room, with a good supper afterward, and for his hospitality I was forever indebted to Ben Sawhill.

Ben got out the champagne, filled three glasses, and gave one to Nela and one to me. He held his up, his face very grave, as he said: "This happy occasion calls for a toast. Not just one that you think of off the cuff, but one you'll remember as long as you live. Do you want to hear it?"

"Of course we do," Nela said.

"Not a legal one, Ben," I said.

He laughed. "This one didn't come from Blackstone. It's from the heart of Ben Sawhill." He cleared his throat. "To love and marriage, to happiness that only love and marriage can bring to us, and to a long and happy life for Mr. and Mrs. William Beeson."

We touched glasses, and once more I thought of him and Sarah, and I couldn't help wondering if he would have been any happier if he had married her. We drank, Nela close to crying; and when Ben left, a little later, she kissed him on the cheek, while he swallowed as if something was wrong with his throat, and looked past her at me.

"Lucky man, Will," he said. "You're a lucky man."

He went out and closed the door. The housekeeper was gone, too, and now there was no sound in the room but the ticking of the clock on the mantel. We looked at each other, both of us suddenly taken with shyness. Then Nela came to me and hugged me.

"You make a handsome bridegroom," she said. "While here I am, without any of the finery a bride should have."

"My fault," I said. "I couldn't wait. I can't make it up to you yet, but I will. I promise."

"I know you will," she said. "I don't have the slightest doubt about anything. I know we're going to have a good life together." She stepped back, looking away from me. "Give me a few minutes, Will. I'll call when I'm ready."

She took the lamp and disappeared into the bedroom. I stood there waiting, hearing her moving about in the other room. Presently she called, "All right, Will."

When I went into the bedroom, I saw that she was in bed, her hair a dark mass against the pillow. I stood there awkwardly, painfully aware of the blood throbbing in all my being, and conscious of the fact that I was breathing so hard I was almost panting.

"Blow out the lamp, Will," Nela said.

When I turned to look at her, I saw that she was laughing

at me. Then the full impact of the step we had taken that day struck me. She was my wife. No one could stop us now. Not Sarah. Not John Mathers. And for a while, as I held Nela, the world held only Nela and me.

In the morning I built a fire and Nela cooked breakfast. After we finished eating, I sat at the table smoking while she did the dishes; then she sat down across from me. There was much about Sarah I had not told Nela, but I told her now because we had to come to a decision sometime between now and tomorrow when we returned to the valley. I told my wife that Sarah had stood upright beside her chair, that she had walked a little, and that she had told me not to get too fond of Nela. I put out my hands in a gesture of futility. "Nela, what can I do?"

Nela listened closely, her forehead furrowed in thought. As I looked at her, I was so stirred by my feeling for her that I could not say a single word. It was first love, but it was real love such as I had never known existed. There would never be anything else like it, like last night and this morning and the few hours we still had together.

Suddenly I found words. "We just can't be separated! If Sarah and your dad won't take us together, we'll leave."

"Oh, darling." She reached out and took my hands. "That's what I want too, but we can't. We've got to do the right thing now or we'll be plagued by our mistake the rest of our lives. No matter what happens, you can't forget your debt to Sarah, and I can't forget that John Mathers is my father."

"Then what can we do?"

"We've got to go along for a while just as we were," she said. "I guess I'm a coward, but I just can't quite bring myself to tell Dad yet. After all, we did act pretty fast."

I was a coward too, as far as Sarah was concerned. "All right, perhaps there'll be a better time," I said.

"Will." She squeezed my hands. "I don't want you to get mad at me, but I'd like to tell you something I think about Sarah. It's not anything I can prove; but because I'm a woman and Sarah is a woman I think I know something about her that you would never think of.''

"Go ahead," I said.

"I think she's been able to walk for a long time." Absolute disbelief must have come into my eyes, for Nela added quickly: "Will, let me finish. I've watched her when she was in her chair and when she didn't think anyone was looking. The way she moves her legs makes me think they're not paralyzed. And the bottoms of her shoes are worn. I know you've said she's been taking a few steps, but I noticed her shoes almost immediately.''

"Slim evidence," I said.

"But remember, Sawhill told you the doctor said there was nothing physically wrong with her. He said she could walk if she had to.''

I pulled my hands from Nela and walked to the back door. I stood there trembling, thinking that if what Nela said was true, Sarah was a different woman than I had thought for eight years, a woman who had hidden herself from all of us.''

"It's crazy!" I said. "She wouldn't exile herself to a wheel chair for four years.''

"She might," Nela said. "We don't know she told you the truth about her accident. Will, she's a terribly possessive woman; she must have a person's love completely centered on her. Like Dogbone's. And María's. She wants yours. That's why she doesn't want you to love me. I'm her rival, and she's known it for a long time. But she doesn't love you the way I do. Maybe her love is like a mother's. Or a sister's. I don't know. All I know is that she doesn't want to share your love with anyone else.''

I turned, hot words on my tongue, but I didn't say them. Nela was hurrying on. "Joe Pardee must have been a very strong character. So is Sarah. What happened when they got married was bound to happen. Each of them tried to remake the other, or at least prove to be the stronger. Perhaps, because Joe won, Sarah had this accident on purpose.''

"Nela, of all the wild—"

"Wait, Will. I'm still not done. What you haven't thought

about is that a crippled person in a wheel chair has everyone's sympathy. Like Sawhill's. And Dad's. When Dad came home last fall that's all he could talk about. How, though Sarah was an invalid, she was still a beautiful woman who had not let her condition break her spirit.''

I didn't say that what Nela thought was crazy now. I'd had the same feeling many times: A broken body but not a broken spirit. It could be true. Maybe Sarah had driven Joe to Kathy Morgan; but all the time she was punishing Joe, and had never let him forget it. But if she was that possessive, she was cruel, and evil, and somehow I couldn't believe it of her.

"I don't know," I said. "Even if what you think is true, I can't just walk off and leave her. Anyhow, half the ranch is mine."

"I know you can't leave her." She rose and came to me. "Darling, you don't hate me for what I've said? It's something we've got to face just as we have to face my father's weaknesses."

"I couldn't hate you," I said. "I love you." I kissed her and held her in my arms, and never wanted to let her go.

In the morning we started back to Easter Valley, to try to live without each other.

Chapter Twenty-Two

WHILE NELA AND I WERE IN CANON CITY, AL ROMIG DIED suddenly of a heart attack. Nela returned in time to attend the funeral, but neither Sarah nor I heard about it until the following Sunday, when Mathers and Nela came to dinner.

I had often wondered about Mathers, and now that he was my father-in-law I wondered more than ever. He had lost himself in a dream, lost himself so completely that he wasted his private fortune upon it. At first I had respected him for his seeming honesty and sincerity; but recently I had begun to question his motives, partly because of little things Nela had said about him, but mostly because I felt that the real John Mathers was disguised by a fine flow of words and an impressive personality.

I had just about decided that Mathers did not really think in terms of doing good for fifty families, the goal he had expressed so many times. Rather, I thought, prestige and position were most important to him. In St. Louis he had been a hardware merchant, and a prosperous one, but still a small man in a large community. He had changed all that by coming here, where he was a leader who could force his will upon others; and even now, when the clouds of disaster could not be ignored, he still refused to admit they were gathering overhead.

Nela would not have agreed I was right any more than I would have agreed she was right about Sarah, but I realized it was possible for a person to be so close to someone he loved that he could not make an objective judgment. That was the way it had been with me and Joe Pardee. Now that he had been dead for nearly a year, I still wasn't sure I knew what kind of man he really had been.

As far as Mathers' feeling for Al Romig was concerned, I could not question his honest grief. "He was more than a friend," Mathers said at dinner. "He believed in our idea. He supported me in every way he could. I never saw a man work as hard for a principle he believed in as Al did. It was that way right from the start. He came with me last fall because he felt it was his duty, not because he wanted to." Mathers paused to glare at me. "You almost scared him to death when you stopped us below Alton's Trading Post last fall. He was actually physically sick for two days afterward."

Mathers looked down at his plate. "I suppose many heroes live and die and are buried in unmarked graves, and are never mentioned in history. That's the way it was with Al. He was a hero. He wasn't strong enough for a rough country like this. He knew it, but he came because he felt it was something he had to do, and he died because he obeyed the call of duty."

Nela and I got out of the house and down the slope to the willows as soon as we could. We were in each other's arms the instant we were hidden from the eyes of Sarah and Mathers. We hadn't seen each other since Wednesday, and it seemed half a lifetime ago.

There was something else that meant more to Nela than to me, and she mentioned it at once. "It looks as if we're doing something wrong, coming here so furtively. But we're married, Will. It's not as if we were having a clandestine meeting, or being terribly wicked, but I know that's what Sarah's thinking."

Nela was probably right about Sarah, but whether she was or not, there was the question of what we should do and when. I asked, "Do you want to tell them now?"

She shook her head. She was sitting up, hugging her legs, with her chin on her knees as she stared at the creek. "Not

today. Dad's all wrapped up in Al's death. He couldn't stand
another blow. And it will be. We might as well face facts.
It'll be just as hard on Sarah. She doesn't suspect?''

"I don't know what she suspects,'' I said. ''I haven't talked
to her much lately. She didn't ask why I went to Canon City.
She just looks at me accusingly, with her lips tight. It isn't
like her.''

"What *would* be like her, having you obey every whim
and fancy she has?''

"I guess so,'' I said. ''What about your dad?''

She laughed shortly. ''He's so wrapped up in his colony
affairs that he never thinks of me. It will be like hitting him
with a club when we tell him.''

"For a while I thought they really were in love with each
other,'' I said. ''Now it's beginning to fade.''

"It's been fading for quite a while,'' Nela said. ''Sarah is
tired of listening to Dad. He doesn't talk about her. Maybe
she's found out he doesn't respond to her touch the way she
thought he would. Or maybe she's worrying so much about
you that she hasn't got room for anyone else.'' Nela looked
at me. ''Oh, Will, I love you so much!''

I took her into my arms, finding it hard to say what was
in my heart. ''I love you, too. Don't let anything ever happen
that will separate us.''

"I won't. I promise, darling.''

We walked back to the house, each trying to be sedate and
to look unconcerned about the other, and both of us feeling
like the hypocrites we were. Before we reached the house,
Nela said: ''Dillingham is still working for Turner. What are
they waiting for?''

"I don't know,'' I said.

The natural guess was that they intended to clean the range
of Anchor cattle and sell them and pocket the money, but
that was Mathers' business. Nothing I could do or say would
prevent it happening. He wouldn't believe anything I told
him.

"The gossip is that Dillingham spends a lot of time with
Kathy Morgan,'' Nela said.

"Turner?''

"He goes there, too, I guess," she said, "but he's with the colonists most of the time. He keeps telling them that all they've got to do is to move onto your range to get their quarter-section of land. Some of them are listening, too. The grain isn't maturing, you know." She smiled at me. "That makes you a good prophet, husband."

"I didn't have to be smart to prophesy that," I said. "Does your dad know?"

"He must." She shook her head, frowning. "But he ignores it, as he does everything he doesn't want to happen."

After they left, I sat on the porch, with Sarah beside me in her wheel chair. It was the first time we had been alone together for a long while. She looked across the valley to the Sangre de Cristo range, now almost bare of snow. She murmured, "It's beautiful, isn't it, Will?"

"Yes," I said, "but I thought you hated it."

"I hate my memories," she said. "Not the valley."

The evening was pleasantly warm, with the smell of rain in the air. Shadows were long, and the scarlet glory of sunset was at its peak above the mountains. Time was rushing by, I thought. Fall roundup and the yearly drive to Leadville, then winter, and, unless I did something, I would still have no wife beside me.

I stood up and looked down at Sarah, but she ignored me as she had been doing for days. She *knows*, I thought. I saw lines in her forehead and around her eyes. Her hands, loosely clasped on her lap, looked very fragile.

"When are you going to marry Mathers?" I asked.

"I don't know," she said listlessly.

"Trouble's still coming," I said. "We'll have colonists squatting on Box P grass within a month."

She said, still not looking at me: "We've had too much trouble already, Will. I'd rather lose the Box P than take a life."

I turned and walked away, past the cottonwoods and on to the corral, where I roped and saddled my horse. I rode to Kathy Morgan's place, stirred by the need for action. The waiting had stretched out too long already, and I wasn't sure

I could go on waiting. I felt like a boiling tea kettle with the lid tightly closed and a potato over the spout. Something would give if I found Dillingham with Kathy.

When I tied my horse in front of Kathy's house, twilight had become night. I checked my gun carefully, then went up the path and, crossing the porch, knocked on her front door. It was too dark for her to have seen me ride up, but she would have heard me. I knocked again, and a third time, the last very hard. A moment later I heard steps; then the lock turned and Kathy opened the door.

I said, "You're getting deaf, Kathy."

She was wearing a dark blue robe over a flannel nightgown; her hair was hanging down her back, and from the hard set of her mouth I saw that a black mood was upon her. Though the lamp was behind her, so that her face was shadowed, there was no doubt about her temper.

"I was in bed," she said. "You're a fool to come here, Will."

I wasn't sure why I was there except that I had acted on impulse, feeling that I had to do something and half hoping that Dillingham would be there so that I could kill him. Now I was convinced he was in Kathy's house, probably in the bedroom she had just left.

"You're sick?" I asked.

"No."

She stood in front of me, waiting to hear what had brought me, her body blocking the doorway. Suddenly I was struck by the difference in her. She had always welcomed me before, even going out to the road to call me in. Now she just stood there, waiting; and for some reason she struck me as being wicked. I couldn't have defined her wickedness unless it was that she had intended using me, and, having failed, had no more use for me.

"God damn it, Will, what do you want?" she demanded.

I lunged forward, knocking her arm out of the way, and jerked the door from her grip and slammed it shut. I asked, in a low voice, "Where's Dillingham?"

"I don't know."

"When did you see him last?"

"Two months ago."

"Have you seen Merle Turner?"

"No." She licked her lips, suddenly wary. "Did you get that star I told you to?"

"No." I glanced at the bedroom door, then brought my gaze back to her. "This is a different welcome than I usually get. Why?"

Her black expression began to lighten. She said: "You had every chance, Will, but you didn't want it. That's all the answer you need."

"I guess so," I said, sensing that back of her words was more feeling than she was willing to express. I could have filled the void Joe's death had left, but I had wanted no part of it. "Kathy, Sarah says that Joe made her ride Prince the time she had her accident and that he was to blame for her being crippled."

I had intended to ask this for a long time. Though I didn't want to think Sarah had lied to me, I'd found it hard to believe Joe was capable of doing anything as utterly cruel as that had been. He must have told Kathy his version of what had happened, and if Nela was right about Sarah, Joe's side of it might be the truth. I watched Kathy's face closely; I saw astonishment, and then she laughed.

"Sounds like her," she said. "Well, you go back and tell your respectable, pious widow that she's a God-damned liar! She was on her mare. She made Joe race with her. He didn't want to because he was on Prince, and he knew Prince was a hell of a lot faster than the mare. She was losing, and trying to get more speed out of the mare than the animal had when the mare hit a badger hole and took a spill." She opened the front door, whispering: "Now get out. Quick! Come back later if you want to."

The bedroom door opened a thin crack, just enough for a gun barrel to slip through. I'd found Dillingham. I was sure of that; but I wasn't nearly as anxious to see him as I had thought I was—not with him having the drop on me like this.

I lunged through the door and across the porch and made

a wide swing around the yard to the hitching pole; I mounted and went back up the road on the run. Then, realizing how close to death I had been, sweat broke out all over me. Kathy Morgan had saved my life.

Chapter Twenty-Three

NELA REACHED THE END OF HER STRING ON THE SUNDAY afternoon before we started fall roundup. The day was a cold one, too cold to be comfortable outside. The previous week had left the first frosting of snow on the peaks of the Sangre de Cristos, and I had found a skim of ice on the horse troughs each morning. The aspens on both sides of the valley were bright patches of orange, and even here, along the creek, the cottonwood and willow leaves were turning, a few falling so that they made a dry rustling under our feet.

Nela pounded the dirt with a closed fist, crying out at me: "I can't go on, Will! It isn't any way to start a marriage! By the time you get back from Leadville, there won't even be enough leaves on the brush to hide us. Are we doing this because we don't want to hurt Sarah and Dad, or because we're cowards?"

"Both, I guess," I said. "I'm a bigger coward when it comes to Sarah than anything else."

"I know," Nela said bitterly. "You always think of her first, but it's time you were thinking of yourself. And me."

She had a right to be bitter. Maybe we should have cut every tie the day we returned from Canon City. I still wasn't sure, but from Nela's tone of voice I knew we couldn't put it off any longer.

"All right," I said. "Let's go tell them now."

She looked at me to see if I meant it. "You're sure you want to?"

"No, but it's got to be done."

"What will she do?"

"I don't know. She can't fire me and she can't run me off, because I'm half-owner. And she won't go to your dad."

"He knows that," she said. "Their affair was like a fire-cracker that just sputtered out. I guess they never did really love each other."

"Well, we've got to face facts," I said. "Sarah won't want another woman in the house with her. Or, even if she says she's willing, she'd make it impossible for you to stay."

"I'm sure she would," Nela agreed.

"So we've got one of two things to do. We can build another house and I can go on rodding the Box P, or we can cut loose and start somewhere else."

"I'm not afraid," she said. "We'll cut loose."

I rose and helped her to her feet. I kissed her and held her for a moment, and for that moment I could not speak. I loved her too much. I was lucky, just as Ben Sawhill had said on the day we were married, to get Nela; lucky to be loved by her, and lucky that I hadn't married some other woman. But because it was hard for me to say things like that, I just held her in my arms and looked at her, hoping she could see in my eyes what was in my heart.

Nela smiled and said, "Let's go beard the lion and lioness in their den."

We walked up the slope together, her arm through mine, for now we didn't care what they saw or said. Just before we reached the house, I said: "There is one thing. I'll be gone for two or three weeks, depending on luck and weather. You'd better stay with your dad until I get back."

"Of course," she said. "I wouldn't fit on roundup very well."

We went in. Mathers was in the middle of one of his monologues. Sarah sat by the window sewing, plainly bored. There had been a time when she was impressed by him and hung on every word, but that time had been long gone. These

Sunday-afternoon dinners had become habit as much as anything.

Mathers stopped, irritated by our entrance. We had not been gone as long as usual. "Get cold?" he asked.

"Yes," Nela said, "but that isn't why we came back. We have something to tell you."

Sarah laid her sewing in her lap, stuck the needle through the cloth, and looked at me. I think she expected to hear we were engaged, which would still have given her time to break us up.

I said, "Nela and I were married in Canon City last month."

Sarah's face went deathly white. A cry came out of her as if she were choking; then she whirled her chair around and wheeled it into the bedroom as fast as she could and slammed the door. Only then did I look at Mathers. He surprised me by crossing the room and holding out his hand.

"Congratulations," he said. "I should have foreseen this, but I didn't. I have only one thing to say. You're getting the finest girl in the world, and I hope you prove worthy of her."

"I aim to," I said.

Nela kissed him then, and began to cry. "I was afraid you wouldn't feel this way," she said, and sat down and wiped her eyes. "I've told Will I hate weepy women, but I guess I've been worrying about this too long."

Mathers patted her awkwardly on the head, then walked to the window and took out his pipe and began to fill it. "To tell the truth, I don't quite know how to take it. If you had said you were going to get married, I'd have had a little time to adjust myself; but now I find I already have a son-in-law, and, I suppose, a grandchild on the way."

"No, but I hope you will soon," Nela said quickly.

"I knew you would want it that way," he said, "and it's right and proper. But it presents a problem, Beeson. As Nela has probably told you, I cannot help you financially. So my question is a natural one. How will you be able to support a family?"

"I have a little money," I said. "If I don't stay here, I'll get a job." Irritated, I added, "We never expected to live off you."

He didn't act as if he had heard me. He stared at his pipe, his face troubled, and now his thoughts seemed to turn inward. "I'll lose my housekeeper," he said. "She's a good one, Beeson, a very good one. So that makes you the winner in every field of action."

I said, "You didn't expect Nela to stay with you all her life, did you?"

"No, of course not. I wasn't thinking of that. You have called me your enemy. Unfortunately, you have been proved right in your predictions. Our crops did not mature. Perhaps it was the season, but the fact stands. Over half of our people are gone. Only the farmers are left besides me and Scott. There is talk of moving onto your range and Costello's and Brahms's. Those who are doing the talking are men who will vote to dissolve the society and divide our assets."

"I'm sorry—" I began.

"No, you're not sorry because you have been proved right, and no man is sorry in a case like that. . . . But now you are taking from me the only person who is vital to me, so I am very much alone. It will be an effort to adjust myself. As for my promise to keep my people off your range, I will keep it if I live." He glanced at the bedroom door. "However, there is a possibility you will no longer be connected with the Box P."

"I'm half-owner," I said.

"One house and two women?" He shook his head. "It would never do."

He lighted his pipe casually, and some of my old respect for him returned. Though he had admitted he was on the brink of disaster, he still retained an air of dignity and confidence. In spite of all that had happened, I found myself feeling pity for the man.

"Then we'll find another way," I said. "Nela and I know the difficulty. She'll live with you until I get back from roundup; then we'll decide what we have to do."

"I see." He took his pipe out of his mouth and tamped the tobacco down, strain showing in his face for the first time.

"Beeson, a rumor has come to me that Turner and Dillingham have stolen all of our cattle and sold them. I don't know how to ascertain the truth. Turner might do a thing like that, but I find it hard to believe that he would. I have three other men working on the ranch, but they swear they know nothing about it." He looked at me helplessly. "How do you learn the truth in a case like this?"

"You comb the range," I said. "In your case you'll have to hire men to do it, men you can trust."

"Will you do it?"

"No. Not till I get back, anyway. Why don't you send for the sheriff?"

"Would the sheriff come on the basis of a mere rumor?" He shook his head. "Besides, it would become public knowledge, and I can't afford that as long as the society has a semblance of unity."

There was a moment of silence, Nela sitting with her hands tightly clasped, her face pale. She had not told me this.

Finally her father said: "Suppose you can't stay here and our cattle have been stolen, but next spring we could get back into business—take a herd on shares or borrow money to do so. Would you run Anchor for us?"

"No," I told him. "You don't have a spread any more. Just summer range and your buildings. Your hay land and winter range are gone, some of it plowed up."

"I understand," he said heavily. "Beeson, people say I am too impractical, and I'm afraid they're right. You see, I believed in an ideal so strongly that I overlooked today and had my eyes on tomorrow. So, for Nela's sake, I'm glad you're a practical man. . . . Well, I guess we'd better go. Tell Sarah we will not be here next Sunday, although very likely she knows that."

I went outside with them; and when Mathers stepped up into the seat of the buggy I kissed Nela, and she whispered, "I'll see you as soon as you get back?"

I said, "The minute I get back."

I stayed there as long as I could see them, and then returned to the house, walking slowly. Sarah would be back in the front room, I was sure, and I would be in for it. She was there, but she didn't reproach me as I expected. She sat by the window, her eyes red, a wadded-up handkerchief on her lap.

"Sit down, Will," she said. "I have something important to say to you." I obeyed, and she went on in a cool tone: "I am going to write to Ben to take charge of my business. You will stop in Canon City when you get back from Leadville. You will turn over all the ranch money to him. He will take out the expenses and divide the balance. You will bring $500 of my money to me. What you do with yours is your business. Then you will pack up and leave, and that will be the end of our partnership."

She didn't look at me. She stared out of the window at the broad expanse of the valley, her face very pale. She was suffering. I did not doubt it. A hard word would make her cry again; but self-pity was the source of her misery, and that was a luxury with which I had little patience.

Suddenly, surprisingly, I discovered I had no sympathy for her despite the debt I owed her. John Mathers, though he had failed, had at least reached for something. I could respect a man who had once possessed a worthy dream. But there was no sensible explanation of Sarah's behavior.

I thought about the day I had first seen Sarah, when I was trying to hide in the creek and Sarah laid down the clothes she had brought and told me to put them on. I still did not understand that, and I did not understand her now, sitting there and looking out of the window, as unconcerned about breaking up our relationship as she had been about my nakedness when I was in the creek.

Maybe the answer was that she considered me a chattel, that I belonged to her just as Dogbone did. The day would come when she would lose him too; I wondered what she would do then.

"You can go," she said. "That's all I have to say."

"I'm not going," I said. "You can give half a ranch away, but you're forgetting you can't take it back after it's given."

"No, I'm not forgetting. I don't believe you'll insist on staying. You'll receive half of what the ranch has made this year along with your regular wages, and that is all you can expect. You also know I will not tolerate Nela in my house; if you want to live with her, you will take her somewhere else.''

She must hate Nela, I thought, as much as she hates Kathy Morgan. I said, ''You still need me.''

''I will find another foreman as good as you are,'' she answered.

''Are you going to let the colonists move in?''

''I'll stop them.''

''Then you'll need me.''

''The world is full of men who know how to pull a trigger.''

The words didn't sound like her, but I was beginning to see that she could shed an attitude as easily as she could take off her coat. I said, ''I suppose you'll be marrying John Mathers soon.''

The question jarred her. ''Of course not!'' She looked at me sharply. ''He's just like Joe even if he talks a different language. With you it's your wife. With John it's his foolish colony. With Joe it was the ranch. I won't share my men with anything or anybody. You should know that by now.''

So there it was at last, honestly said in her own words.

I rose, my mind made up. ''According to the Good Book,'' I said, ''a man should be unselfish, but I'm not. I've got a wife to support. I'm holding on to what I've got.''

I walked out, leaving her sitting there, and hating me, I suppose, just as she had hated Joe Pardee.

Chapter Twenty-Four

THE ROUNDUP AND DRIVE TO LEADVILLE WENT AS SMOOTHLY as ever, but when I left the other riders at Alton's Trading Post to go to Canon City, Irv Costello said: "Better get a move on, Beeson. You'll have work to do when you get back."

"What kind of work?"

"Another driving job. You don't think them plow pushers will miss a chance like this, do you, with all of us out of the valley like we've been for the last week?"

"I reckon not," I said. As I wheeled my horse away from the rest, I said to Curly King and Red Thurston: "I'll be home tomorrow afternoon. Don't do anything till I get there."

They nodded agreement, and I rode away, strongly tempted to ignore Sarah's orders and return to the valley with them. Trouble had been foreshadowed from the day Joe Pardee died. Maybe the colonists would never have come to the valley if Joe had lived. Or if Merle Turner had not described the valley in such glowing terms to Mathers. Or if Sarah had not encouraged Mathers.

History, my father used to remark, is a series of causes and effects. He would slap me on the back as he said: "We want to get rich. That's the cause, so we'll go to Santa Fe and get rich. That's the effect."

He had been facetious; but I wasn't, as I thought about the past year. If any of the causal factors had been different, then the following effects would have been changed. But if they had been, I wouldn't be married to Nela. So there it was, the sweet and the bitter.

Eric Brahms's tally had been short this fall. Naturally, he blamed the settlers. Costello had fanned his temper until it was ready to burst into flame. As for Costello, he had been in a hanging mood for weeks. If trouble did start, it might not stop until Mathers and Scott and all of them on the West Fork were dead or driven from the country. And Nela was with her father.

By the time I reached Canon City, I was in a torment of worry, but there comes a time when flesh reaches the end of its endurance, even under the quirting of the spirit. I weighed the eventualities and decided I had ample time. Costello would not move by himself. The others, including Brahms, would hesitate before attacking the colonists' settlement. Though my decision was forced upon me by compelling weariness, I hoped I was right.

I left my horse at a livery stable, rubbed him down myself, ordered a double feeding of oats, and then wearily climbed the stairs to Ben Sawhill's office. He said, "How are you, Will?" and shook hands with me, but I sensed at once that he was not his usual cordial self.

I was too tired to be tactful. I asked, point-blank, "What's wrong, Ben?"

"I was going to ask you that." He motioned to a chair. "Sit down."

I gave him the money I had brought from Leadville and sprawled into the chair. "Sarah told me to turn this over to you. You're to figure the profit, I guess."

"And divide it." He ran a hand through his rumpled hair. "That's what I was going to ask about. I thought you and Sarah would never have a falling out, but she writes that she's dissolving the partnership."

"You want to know the trouble?"

"That's what I'm asking."

"Nela and I told her we got married the day before we started roundup."

Sawhill leaned back in his chair, puzzled. "What's that

got to do with it? I mean, Sarah shouldn't object to your getting married."

"No, but she does." I motioned to the desk. "Go ahead. Do your figuring. I guess Sarah doesn't trust me."

I slept in my chair until he woke me. He had put the money into several canvas sacks. One he would deposit in the bank for Sarah, another was my share, and a third held the $500 I was to take to Sarah.

I got to my feet, a little groggy. I said: "Ben, Sarah gave me half the Box P. I'm going to hang onto that."

He got up from his swivel chair, put his hands on the desk, and leaned forward. "Better think that over, Will. You came to the Box P empty-handed. You've had a home for eight years, a job that paid you well, and now you've just been given half of the Box P's profit for the past year, and you've already received your regular wages. That's more than fair, man."

"You've been reading Sarah's letter," I said, "but you don't add it up right. I aim to hang onto what's mine and fight for it. If I don't, she won't have anything."

As I walked to the door, he called out, "What in Heaven's name is happening, Will?"

I leaned wearily against the door casing. "Ben, Sarah Pardee is not the unselfish woman we have always thought she was. She's small and self-centered—"

"Stop it!" He broke in as if I had been guilty of blasphemy. "Stop it!" He started toward me, his hands fisted. "Have you gone daft, Will? After all she's done for you—"

"You'll love her, no matter what you find out about her?" I asked.

"Of course! I'll never change, but—"

"Maybe you should pay a visit to the Box P," I said. "She's not going to marry John Mathers. And while you're there, give her some advice. She'll have to get along with me as a partner, or sell out to me. I think she'd better sell. She hates the Box P, but it's different with a man. He becomes a part of the ranch and it becomes a part of him. Maybe you can make her understand that."

From Sawhill's office I went to the bank, barely reaching

it before closing time, and deposited my money. Then I asked to see the president, and arranged for the backing I would need to buy Sarah's share of the ranch.

I didn't know whether Sarah would sell, but I had a hunch that Sawhill would go to the Box P and that Sarah would turn to him just as she had turned to John Mathers a year ago. He was different from Mathers. Because he had no great obsession, except his love for Sarah, he would be the right man for her. I had thought so for a long time.

I had a meal in the hotel dining room, took a room, and went to sleep at once, sprawling across the bed with my clothes on. I was in the saddle on my way out of town before dawn, not even taking time for breakfast. When I rode out of Easter Canyon, I took the shortest way to the ranch that I could, angling across the hills.

I was home hours earlier than either Curly or Red could have expected me, but they had been watching, and they were saddled up by the time I rode into the yard. As I swung down, Curly said: "That animal's about finished. Want me to saddle Roanie for you?"

"What's up?"

"Four of 'em," Red said. "Crossed the line three days ago. Tore down your sign. Starting to put up cabins."

I stood there, one hand wrapped around the saddle horn. There was a fine rain in the air, hardly more than a mist. It would be snowing upon the Sangre de Cristos. Perhaps it would be snowing here in a few hours. I wiped a hand across my face. It came away wet.

Funny, the way I felt inside. Here it was, the thing I had known would happen. I had told myself what I would do. I had told Sarah and Mathers and my crew. Yet now I wanted no part of it.

I looked at Red, at his big nose and freckles and sharp blue eyes that seemed to be asking what we were waiting for. He was my age. Then I glanced at Curly, who was three years younger, and still a kid, to me. Now he began shuffling, impatient.

I looked at the house and thought of Sarah. No, even though I wanted no part of it, I had to do it just the same: *I had no choice.* There would be women and kids down there, and somebody would get hurt, but still I had no choice. I wondered if that was the way Joe Pardee had started.

"They won't be expecting you for another five, six hours," Red said. "I told 'em you'd gone to Canon City but that they'd better look out when you got back."

His words irritated me. He had had no business saying anything to them. That was my job. I said, "You boys don't have to go."

Red flared back, "We don't want to hear no more of that crazy talk."

"All right," I said. "Saddle Roanie. Just be sure you don't start the trouble. I'll start it."

I walked to the house. Sarah was sewing near the window. She looked at me warily, as if not certain what I would say or do. She asked, "Did you see Ben?"

"I saw him." I tossed the money on the couch. "There's your $500."

"Thank you, Will. You can pack up—"

"Sarah," I said, "I'm not packing up. Either we go on being partners, or I'll buy you out. I can raise the money if you don't set an unreasonable price on your half of the ranch and stock." I turned toward the door.

"Where are you going?" she asked.

"I've got a chore to attend to."

She guessed then, and cried out, "No, Will, no! I don't want you killed!"

But I went out of the house and crossed the muddy yard to where Roanie stood saddled and waiting. I asked, "Who are they?"

"The first wagon belongs to Merle Turner," Red said. "The other three belong to Secore— he's a bachelor—and Troy and Runyan. Troy's got a wife and kids. Runyan's just got a wife."

The Anchor crew that had been with Turner and Dillingham all summer. I asked, "How about Gene Dillingham?"

"He ain't around," Curly said.

"The hell he's not," I said, and swung into the saddle, my Winchester in the boot.

We left in a gallop, mud splattering behind us. Sarah, standing in the doorway, screamed, "Will! Come back! Will!"

I pretended not to hear.

Chapter Twenty-Five

MERLE TURNER'S WAGON WAS NOT FAR DOWNSTREAM FROM the pool where Nela and I had spent so many of our Sunday afternoons. He was not in sight. Neither were his horses, but a campfire was burning between the wagon and the creek.

I hesitated, a prickle running down my spine: he might be back in the brush taking a bead on me now. But Red had told him I wouldn't be back until evening, so maybe he'd cooked a meal here, then gone downstream to one of the other camps.

I was balancing the possibilities in my mind when Curly said: "Secore's got his cabin started. Turner might be down there."

I nodded and swung to the ground. "Keep your eyes peeled," I said, and, gathering a handful of burning sticks, tossed them into the wagon. I had started to pick up some more, but then I saw it wasn't necessary. Inside, a straw tick had caught and blazed up.

I stepped into the saddle, saying, "Better move."

We went down the road on the run. I saw the smoke of Secore's campfire, then his wagon as we rounded a turn, the outfit at the other end of a straight stretch. A pile of peeled logs lay on the bank above the creek. Secore was notching one of them. Turner was on the other side of him, using a draw knife.

They didn't hear us coming until I fired a shot over their

heads and yelled: "Harness up! You're rolling. Move! Move!"

Secore jumped toward his rifle leaning against a wagon wheel, but he didn't make it. Red threw a shot that splintered a spoke next to the rifle barrel. Secore fell flat on his belly and lay there, his hands palm down in the mud.

But Turner was another story. He dropped his draw knife and pulled his gun. I fired and hit him in the side, the bullet turning him partly around, but he held onto his gun and took a shot at me, the bullet slicing through my coat just above my left shoulder. We were close then, all three of us shooting at him. He was driven back on his heels and on down to the ground, dead before he fell.

I reined up and dismounted. Secore hadn't moved, probably thinking I was going to shoot him. I kicked him in the ribs. Not hard. Just enough to make him grunt. "Up!" I said. "On your feet."

He struggled to his hands and knees and turned his head far enough to see me and the gun in my hand; then he turned his head the other way and saw Red and Curly and the guns in their hands and he fell belly-flat into the mud again.

"Put up your guns," I told Red and Curly. "Haul him to his feet."

They did, shoving Secore back against the wheel. He whimpered as he gripped the tire behind him.

"You're a stout one," I said. "Didn't you think of this when Turner talked you into it?"

"No." He wiped a sleeve across his mouth. "We figured on you coming tonight. We was gonna set a trap at his wagon."

"Cut us down from the back," I said. "The four of you. That right?"

"That's right. Had a sure-fire deal. Turner and Dillingham was gonna pay us $1,000 apiece if we got all three of you."

Rage took hold of me then, and the red haze that swept in front of my eyes was so thick I could hardly see the man. I cocked my gun, and my voice came out harsh and strained. "Any reason I shouldn't kill you?"

"It wasn't me." He pressed back as hard as he could

against the wagon wheel. "Wasn't me at all. It was Turner and Dillingham."

Red reached out and forced my gun down. "You can't kill him, Will. Not that way."

I shook my head, and the haze disappeared. I asked, "Where's Dillingham?"

"I don't know. So help me, I don't know. He pulled out this morning, but he was gonna be at Turner's wagon tonight."

I stared at him. Sweat poured down his face. I couldn't tell whether he was lying or not. Then he said, "Maybe he's in town." He swallowed. "But I—I think he's at Kathy Morgan's."

I still held the gun, thinking that what he said was probably the truth; but apparently he thought he hadn't told me enough. He pointed a trembling finger at Turner's body. "He's got a money belt. It's filled with gold he got from Anchor cattle this summer, him and Dillingham. I mean, he's got his share on him."

I eased down the hammer of my gun and holstered it. "Harness up," I said. "Give him a hand, Red."

I walked through the mud to Turner's bullet-riddled body, unlatched his money belt, and jerked it free. Heavy! John Mathers was luckier than he had any right to be.

"Red, you ride alongside Secore," I said. "Keep him rolling. If he makes a bad move, plug him."

"Not me," Secore said. "I've got my bellyful of this country."

"You're going down the canyon," I said. "All of you. Tonight. If you ever come back, you'll swing. Savvy that?"

"I ain't coming back."

I jerked my head at Curly and we mounted. Troy's outfit was next. We found his wife and children, but no man. "Where is he?" I asked Mrs. Troy.

She had heard the shooting and had gathered the children around her. She hovered over them like a mother hen, staring at me and refusing to answer. Suddenly it struck me that she had probably been one of those in church the morning I had attended with Sarah and had thought the colonists were good people.

"Merle Turner is dead," I said. "Secore is hooking up his team, and he'll be along in a minute. He told me Turner and the rest, including your husband, aimed to set a trap for me and my men tonight and murder us. Does that sound like your husband?"

She looked at me, but only for a moment. "No," she said in a low tone. "Nothing's like him any more. He's listened to Turner too long."

"I don't want to kill him, but I will if I have to," I said. "All I want is for you to get out of the valley and stay out. Where is he?"

"In town," she said. "With Runyan."

I believed her. I asked, "Can you drive your team?"

"Yes," she said.

"Harness up for her," I told Curly. "Throw their stuff into the wagon." I motioned to some odds and ends on the ground. What kind of men were Troy and Runyan, I wondered, who had time to go to town with a cabin not even started and winter at hand? Then, as I mounted, the answer came to me. *They had never planned to make their homes here.* They intended to take the money Dillingham and Turner were going to give them to murder me and Red and Curly and get out of the country. Well, John Mathers had picked up some beauties to build his Great Tomorrow.

"Ride alongside her," I ordered Curly, and as I started downstream I looked back and saw that Secore was in the road, Red riding beside him.

Mrs. Runyan was neither frightened nor defiant. She just seemed resigned. She looked at me, a big bony woman, her hands on her hips. She said: "You want us to pull out. That it?"

"That's it," I said.

"I heerd the shooting," she went on, "so I've been packing up. I knowed it wouldn't work. I told Runyan that, but no, he had to listen to that no-good Dillingham and Windy Turner. We should of trusted Mr. Mathers and stayed where we was. Had a purty good forty. I raised some garden sass on it last summer. Would o' done better, too, if Runyan had helped me instead o' taking it into his head he was a cowpuncher and rode off up there to that old ranch."

I helped her hook up, and by that time Secore and Mrs. Troy were not far behind. I said: "I'm going after Runyan and Troy. You're taking your wagon down the canyon and you're going to keep right on rolling. Do you understand that?"

"I ain't stupid," she said. "Go easy on my man, will you? He ain't much, but he's the best I'll ever get."

We weren't far from Carlton now. I rode back to Curly. "Keep them rolling," I said. "I don't think the women will give you any trouble. I'm going after the two men. I want you and Red to stay with these wagons till they get to the river."

"We'll do it." He grinned at me. "Naw, I don't figure on the women making no trouble for us, and from the looks of 'em, me'n Red won't cause them no trouble."

I whirled Roanie back toward Carlton. If Dillingham was with Kathy Morgan, and saw me, the chances were he'd cut me down from her front door. But I didn't think she'd let him. Anyhow, he wasn't expecting me back until night, so he probably wouldn't be watching.

I was right, at least to the extent that I rode by Kathy's house without anything happening. I crossed the bridge, wondering if Troy and Runyan would give me trouble. Probably not, unless Dillingham was with them. If he was, the odds would be long against me.

Only two horses were hitched in front of Delaney's store, but that might not mean anything. Other horses were tied along the street. I stopped in front of Delaney's and went in. I was lucky. They were both there, standing on opposite sides of the potbellied stove as they talked to Delaney.

They didn't recognize me until I was within ten feet of them. When they did, they were as scared as Secore had been. I said: "Turner's dead. Your wagons are on the way here now. You're leaving the valley today and you're going clear to the river before you stop. If you come back, you can figure on trouble like you've never seen."

"We won't be back," Troy said, and edged toward the door, Runyan following.

Delaney gave me a sneering look. He had backed against the wall to be out of the line of fire if anything broke loose.

"The spirit of Joe Pardee," Delaney said. "I thought it would show up in you before now."

I made a quarter-turn so that I could see him as well as the other two. I said, "You taking it up?"

"Hell, no."

"You don't like it here any more, do you, Art?"

"No. Can't say I do."

"You'd sell out quick if you had a buyer, wouldn't you?"

"Yeah, you bet I would." The sneering expression was replaced by one of greedy interest. "What're you driving at?"

"I'll be back when I get these boys started down the creek," I said, and motioned them toward the door.

I held them outside on their horses, my gun in my hand until their wagons reached town. They tied their horses behind the wagons and got up on the seats with their wives, Mrs. Runyan's tongue beginning to wag before her husband finished tying his horse. They turned down the creek toward the Arkansas, Red and Curly waving at me. I waved back and went into the store.

Chapter Twenty-Six

As I walked to the rear of the store, Delaney stuck his hand into the cracker barrel, grabbed half a dozen, and stuffed them into his mouth. He looked at me speculatively as he chomped. Finally he said, "So you cleared the lice off your range? Locusts, I guess, you used to call them."

"Yeah, they're cleared," I said.

"Costello and Brahms done the same," he said. "Damn' fools, them settlers. Twelve families moved, four to each ranch. If they'd stuck together, and all gone onto one place, they'd have made it go."

I hadn't come back into the store to talk. "Name a price," I said, "on everything you own: store building, stock, and house."

He put another cracker into his mouth, and I could almost smell the greed that was working in him. Finally he said, "Ten thousand."

I started toward the front door. I had almost reached it when I heard him pattering after me. "Hold on, Will." As I turned, he said, "I want to sell, all right. Maybe $10,000 is a mite high, but before I talk turkey I've got a right to know whether you're serious or just bulling me."

"I'm serious," I said, "and there's cash money to swing the deal, but when you talk about $10,000 you're not a mite high. You're ten times high."

"Now, now, Will. I ain't gonna give this property away.

Why, I've got some right nice stained-glass windows in the house—''

"It's the store I'm interested in," I said. "Keep the house and rent it if you want to."

"No. When I leave, I ain't coming back. All right, if you've got cash, $7,500."

I turned around again, but he ran at me and grabbed my arm. "Don't jump your traces, Will. Is it you that's buying? I mean, you quitting the Box P?"

"I don't know," I said, and I honestly didn't.

"You can run a store or rod a ranch," Delaney said, "but you can't do both."

"All right, I can't."

Again I would have walked out if he hadn't hung on to my arm, bracing himself with both legs. "Five thousand."

I shook him off, irritated, and cuffed back my hat. "No good, Art. It boils down to a question of whether you want to sell and get out with a little bit, or walk out with nothing. A lot of us don't cotton much to the way you've sucked around after the settlers. You should have known better."

"They done it wrong," he said sullenly. "If they'd spread out all over the valley and thrown some lead right at first, they'd have whipped you cow nurses good."

"If they had whipped us, it wouldn't have done you any good," I said. "They had their own store and figured on selling stuff at cost. But you couldn't see to the end of your nose." He stared at the floor without saying anything. I said: "Art, I've got $3,000. That's what I'll give you."

He got red in the face, and then white, and I thought he'd faint. Then he howled: "You're a robber, Will Beeson! You're a God-damned robber! Why, the goods on my shelves . . ." I turned to the door for the fourth time, and I was through it and on the porch when his voice came to me, high and shrill, "I'll take it."

"Make out the papers," I said. "I've got some riding to do. I'll stop back later tonight."

I walked through the drizzle to the blacksmith's shop, arranged with Slim Reardon to bring in Merle Turner's body, and then left town, riding against the wind, the desire to see

Nela an overpowering urge in me. The air was colder now. Within an hour or two the drizzle would turn to snow.

My original idea was to put Mathers in the store. Now that I had agreed to buy it, I was tormented by a plague of doubts. I had never been able to find any common ground with Mathers. He probably hated me for taking Nela. After I had time to think, I decided I didn't want to have anything more to do with him than I was forced to by family obligations.

I realized I might feel that way because I was tired and my nerves pulled too tight. I had killed a man, or at least had had a part in it. Whether it was my bullet or Red's or Curly's that finally smashed life out of Merle Turner was something we would probably never know.

Still, I was responsible for it. Killing a man was not an easy thing to forget, even when the man was Merle Turner. Then—and, perversely, I found some pleasure in the thought—it struck me that Mathers was to blame because he promised me that his people would not cross the line onto Box P range.

So, when I reined up in front of Mathers' cabin and dismounted, I was filled with bitterness toward John Mathers, a failure who would not or could not keep a promise. I'd made a mistake. I'd bought a store that I'd have to run myself. A poor living, but a living; being a married man, I had to think of that.

Nela recognized me even in the rapidly thinning dusk, and came flying out of the cabin, disregarding the rain and the mud. "Will, where have you been?" she cried. "I expected you yesterday." She seemed to be all over me, her arms around me, her body against mine, and our lips together.

All the bitterness was flushed out of me then. I felt as if I had been purged of something that was evil and unclean. She was my wife and I loved her, and John Mathers was her father—a futile man, a dreamer, a failure, but still her father.

We went inside, and the warmth from the big range rushed at me. Nela closed the door and began unbuttoning my coat. A lighted lamp was on the table. Next to the wall I saw Lin

Scott, the little schoolteacher and secretary of the colony, sitting in a chair, his legs stretched toward the stove. He rose and came toward me, holding out his hand.

"Congratulations, Beeson," Scott said. "I haven't seen you since I learned of your marriage. Believe me, winning this girl is a great accomplishment. I know, because I've seen some good men try."

"Thanks," I said, and then I looked at the bed on the other side of the room. John Mathers lay on his back, staring at the ceiling, his face bandaged.

"You haven't had anything to eat, have you?" Nela asked as she hung my coat and hat near the stove. "I'll fix you something. We had bread and milk a while ago, but I'll drink a cup of coffee with you."

I said in a low tone to Scott, who was still standing beside me, "What happened?"

"They almost beat him to death," Scott said. "Turner and Dillingham and Secore and that bunch. He tried to stop them, you know. It was while you were out of the valley." He touched his head gingerly. "I tried to help him, but somebody hit me with a gun barrel when it started and I was out of the fight."

Nela came back to me from the stove. "Go over and speak to him, Will. He's been wanting to see you."

I walked to the bed. I looked down at him, and saw that he recognized me at once.

"Hello, Will," he said. "I tried, but I failed. I guess I've failed at everything since I left St. Louis."

I wanted to say something to give him some assurance, but my throat was too fuzzy. I was ashamed, as thoroughly ashamed as a man could be, for the thoughts I'd had a few moments ago about John Mathers.

"I don't think you're a failure, Dad," Nela said.

I found my voice then, and I said: "A man who fights to keep his word is not a failure. John, I've got something for you." I laid Turner's money belt on the bed. "Turner was shot and killed this afternoon. That's his share of the money from the cattle he and Dillingham stole. If Dillingham's still around, we'll get him, too."

He felt the belt with his right hand, but he didn't lift it. He said, "Thank you, Will."

Nela pulled me away from the bed, whispering, "He tires easily, Will."

While she warmed up some food for me, Scott told me what had happened. "Dillingham and Turner and Secore had been talking to our people for weeks. I guess you heard." I nodded, and he went on. "Dillingham didn't carry any weight because he was a valley man to start with, and everybody knew he had it in for you and Mrs. Pardee. It was Turner who did the mischief. A certain group thought everything he said was gospel, and John had trusted Turner from the beginning. We wouldn't have come to this valley if it hadn't been for him. John never believed you about the growing season being too short because Turner told him he'd seen tremendous crops of wheat and oats and potatoes and such.

"Some of our people succeeded in raising a garden, but that was all. Turner kept saying it was an unusual year, but he claimed the only way to make a living was to have at least a quarter-section of land. He blamed John and me for buying Anchor and trying to make a small acreage do for each family. Finally they forced a meeting and voted to dissolve the society and divide the treasure, which amounted to nothing; a share of zero is zero.

"John and me knew it would be close. There were twenty-three families counting me and John. The vote was twelve to eleven, which means nine families were willing to stay right where they were on the West Fork. Well, John lost his head when he saw he was outvoted. He got in the doorway and said he wasn't letting any of them out until they came to their senses and kept the pledge they'd taken when they left St. Louis. They just ran over him. He tried to fight, but there were too many of them."

"How bad is he hurt?"

"His left arm's broken. Besides the cuts on his face, he's got a couple of broken ribs and a lot of bruises."

Nela motioned me to the table and poured coffee for herself and Scott. She said in a low tone: "He's able to sleep. At least, I guess he sleeps. He just lies there almost as if he were in a coma. He says he's ruined everything for me because he couldn't keep his word to you.''

"Don't let him think that," I said. "We'll make out."

"Of course, Will." She put a hand over mine. "That's the last thing I ever worry about."

I hadn't eaten all day, and by the time I was full some of the tiredness had left me. I told them what had happened, and Scott nodded. He said, "The ones who are left will make a living, if Costello and Brahms let them stay."

"They'll let them," I said, and rose. "I've got to get back to the Box P. I'll settle it with Sarah one way or the other, and I'll see you tomorrow."

"I wish you could stay," Nela said. "We haven't known what we were going to do from the day we were married. Sometimes I wonder if I can stand it."

"Tomorrow," I said, and thought how many times Mathers had used the word. "Don't let your dad worry. We're going to figure things out."

"I'm glad you talked to him," she said.

I looked at the long body lying motionless on the bed, and I thought of him trying to stand in that doorway against men like Dillingham and Turner, fighting when he wasn't a fighting man; and then I remembered him walking up the road that April day with a white handkerchief tied to a stick, not knowing whether we would shoot him or not.

"Nela," I said, "he's a brave man. Tell him that. Tell him he belongs in this country. He's just got to find his place in it. That's all."

I put on my hat and coat, and kissed her, and it seemed only a moment I had been with her. "Don't stay up all night," I said. "You're tired."

She nodded at Scott. "Lin spells me off, and his wife comes in part of the time."

She stood in the doorway until I was in the saddle and starting back down the road. I had that picture to carry in my mind, of her standing motionless with the light behind her, of her strong, straight body that would bear my children. She closed the door, and the night blackness was all around me, and the rain that had turned to snow was whipped past me by the wind.

Chapter Twenty-Seven

ORDINARILY DELANEY WOULD HAVE LOCKED THE STORE and gone home hours ago, but he was still there when I reached town, proof that he was anxious to make any kind of sale and get out of the valley. I stomped snow from my boots before I went in.

"Cold night, ain't it?" he said. "Took you a long time." He handed me a sheet of paper. "Sign it and you can go home and I can go to bed."

He had scrawled the words of a simple agreement stating that I would buy his store and house for $3,000, possession to be given and payment to be made within ten days. I signed it and handed it back.

"Got another copy," he said. "One for both of us."

I signed it, too, and folded it and slipped it into my pocket, thinking gloomily that I had been a fool, that after the beating Mathers had taken he would leave the valley, leaving me with a store on my hands. What I knew about storekeeping I could put in my eye.

Delaney had been watching me, and I guess he didn't like my expression. He said, "You try getting out of this, and I'll law you till hell freezes over and I'll law you back—"

At the sound of a shot he broke off. For a moment I wasn't sure where it came from, with the front door of the store closed, but Delaney seemed to know. He said, smugly: "They

was bound to do it sooner or later. I hope they plug each
other. She's been a disgrace to the community. . . .''

I grabbed his fat shoulder and shook him. "Who are you
talking about?"

"Dillingham and that Morgan woman. He's been with her
all day. He started up the East Fork tonight and met Reardon
coming down with Turner's body. Reardon told him what
had happened, and Gene was fit to be tied. Reardon said
Dillingham done the fanciest cussing he had ever heard, and
headed back to the Morgan . . ."

I went out of the store on the run while Delaney was still
talking, untied my horse, and swung into the saddle. This
was the finish. I don't know why I was so sure. Just a feeling,
maybe. But it made sense. Dillingham and Turner had been
working on their scheme all summer. Now Turner was dead
and his friends had been cleaned off Box P range. Dillingham
would be wild, but he should be after me, not Kathy. Maybe
he'd got drunk. The least I could do was to find out. I owed
Kathy that much.

When I reached her house, I saw that the hitch pole was
empty, but a horse had been there a few minutes before. The
front door was open, lamplight blurred by the whirling snow.
I ran to the house, and when I made the step up to the porch
I saw Kathy lying in the center of her front room.

I went in, slamming the door, and knelt beside her. She
was alive, her pulse strong and regular. Blood had trickled
down her forehead and dried, making a brown stain above
her left eye. It wasn't bullet wound; she'd been knocked out
by a blow.

I carried her to the couch. She was beginning to stir. When
I turned toward the kitchen door, I became aware of the
shambles the house had become. Dillingham had taken an ax
and smashed holes in the floor and the wall. Chairs were
upended, drawers jerked out and emptied. The upholstery on
the back of the couch had been ripped by a knife.

I found a dishcloth in the kitchen and wet it at the pump.
The same thing had happened there. Even the pantry had been
emptied; supplies and broken dishes were scattered all over
the kitchen floor. I returned to the front room where, sitting

down beside Kathy, I began to wipe her face, all the while trying to figure out what had hit Dillingham. He was a bully who probably got pleasure out of sheer destruction, but why at Kathy's?

She came out of it within a minute or so. She put a hand to her head, asking, "How bad is it, Will?"

"Just a lump on your head," I told her. "Did he hit you with a gun barrel?"

"Yes. I tried to kill him but I missed. Before I could shoot again, he cracked me. That's all I remember." She licked her lips, still feeling her head. "Get me a drink, Will. There's a bottle in the pantry if he didn't take it."

I found it, and a cup that wasn't broken, went back into the front room, and poured her a stiff drink. She sat up long enough to get it down, then fell back, clutching the top of her head.

"My God, somebody's hitting me with a hammer!" She shut her eyes, closing her left hand into a fist and beating the couch beside her. "The bastard, the damn' lying stealing double-crossing son of a bitch."

"What was he after, Kathy?"

She opened her eyes to look at me, her right hand still holding her head. "You don't know, do you, Will? You really don't know. That damned Dillingham. You can fight something that's in the open, can't you? Like Turner and his clod-busters. You cleaned 'em off Box P range slicker'n a whistle, but you didn't know you'd turn Dillingham into a wild man. You don't savvy anybody who waits and waits, do you? Me and Dillingham were good waiters, for a while. I wanted him to wait some more, but he wouldn't. Had to rob me, and get out, but I'll get him. By God, I'll get him if I chase him to hell and clean across it!"

"What was he after, Kathy?" I asked again.

She motioned to the table. "Give me another drink."

I poured the drink. She took it and handed the cup back. She said: "Money. What else would make him do a thing like this? And after all I've done for him." She swore for a full minute. "I had better'n $4,000 laid away. Saved most of it when Joe was alive and every Saturday night was pay day. Didn't know then what I was saving for, but I knew after Joe cashed in. Left me $1,000 a damned measly $1,000 after me taking care of him the way I done. His wife wasn't any good.'' Kathy waved a limp hand at me. ''No good for you, neither. She bought you with half a ranch just like I knew she'd do. I warned you, Will, and you got huffy about it. Gimme another drink.''

She emptied the bottle, then threw it across the room. ''Sarah wasn't good for nothing or nobody, but she was respectable. She was married. Had a marriage license. A piece of paper to show everybody. But me, I never did. I just took care of her man when she wouldn't. I loved him, Will. But that white-haired lying thing he married didn't. He was gonna leave me all his money, and what'd I get. A thousand dollars!''

She sat up, cursing again as pain racked her, but she'd had enough whisky to make her talk. Even after what had happened tonight, she seemed to hate Sarah far more than she hated Gene Dillingham. She jabbed a forefinger at me.

''You can buy respectability. That's what I was saving for. Had the money right here in the house, and Gene knew it. After you killed Turner, he was bound to pull out of the valley. Wanted me to go with him, but I wouldn't. I was going to stay here and bust your window friend. I'd have hired some gunslingers to do the job—not plow pushers like Secore and Troy and Runyan. We aimed to get you, Will, you and Thurston and the King kid. Run off her cattle. Whittle her down till she'd be glad to sell. I was going to buy the Box P, and then I'd live up there in the house where Joe lived and I'd lord it over the valley just like they used to when Joe was alive.''

She shut her eyes again. I sat there staring at her, thinking that the last time I had seen her I had sensed she was evil; but I hadn't realized how virulent her hatred for Sarah was, how much she had changed in the year since Joe was killed.

I rose. Whatever sympathy I'd had for her in the past was gone. She'd leave the valley. I'd see to it that she did.

She went on. ''Gene hunted till he found the money. That's when I tried to kill him. We figured it out a long time ago.

I was gonna buy the Box P and he was gonna run it for me, and people'd look up to us just like they used to look up to Joe and that thing he married. But Gene wouldn't wait. Now he'll kill her and he'll go 'way with my money...."

I grabbed Kathy by both shoulders and shook her until she cursed me and put her hand to her head again. I yelled: "Where's Dillingham? Did he go to the Box P?"

"Lemme alone. Head hurts." Then she leered at me. "Sure he went to the Box P, 'n' you're too late to stop him. He'll kill her 'n' then he'll kill you. Think he'll forget she made you foreman 'stead of him? Not Gene. No, sir...."

I didn't wait to hear any more. I ran across the snow-covered yard and swung into the saddle once more, the wind still blasting across the valley, fat snowflakes pelting me as I put my tired horse up the road to the Box P. Kathy Morgan's words were going through my mind in an endless burning refrain: *"Sure he went to the Box P, and you're too late to stop him."* She could have told me that at first, but instead she'd talked and talked, holding me there so that Dillingham would have more time.

And if I was too late? No, I couldn't be. All the differences that had accumulated between me and Sarah were nothing, nothing at all.

Chapter Twenty-Eight

THE RIDE FROM FROM KATHY MORGAN'S HOUSE TO THE BOX P was a nightmare. The temperature was dropping; the wind was blowing harder; the snowflakes were bigger than they had been and there were twice as many of them.

The darkness was so complete that I could see absolutely nothing. I gave the horse his head, and terror grew inside me until it became intolerable. A road ran up the creek past the turn-off to the Box P buildings. If the animal followed the road, I'd find myself far up in the Cedar Hills before I realized it, and by the time I got back to the ranch it would be too late to help Sarah.

I tried to grasp at some hope. Maria and Dogbone were home. Maybe they could stop Dillingham. Or maybe Red and Curly had returned after escorting the settlers to the Arkansas River. No, they wouldn't have started back in this storm. As for Maria and Dogbone, Dillingham would shoot them, or knock them in the head. . . .

That was when the nightmare really took hold of me. I couldn't think. Something inside kept telling me to ride, ride . . . and then I couldn't remember why I was riding or what I had to do. All I knew was that it was cold and that it was an effort to stay in the saddle.

My horse stopped. Instinct made me dismount. I knew I could not stand there motionless, so I began stirring around and waving my arms, and a moment later I stumbled into the corral gate. Then it came back to me—Dillingham . . . Sarah . . . what I had to do.

My fingers were stiff. Though I was wearing gloves, my hands were so cold I began beating them together and closing and opening my fists as I circled the yard. I reached the front of the barn and followed it to the opposite corner, then on to the bunkhouse, the hope in me that Dogbone was there and had a good fire going. But the bunkhouse windows were dark, and when I opened the door the room seemed as cold as the driving snow outside.

I went on toward the house, guided by a faint show of light that was hardly anything at all when I first saw it, so hard was it snowing. But it was enough, and now I was fully aware of what lay ahead. I must kill Gene Dillingham or he would kill me. The waiting was over, and yet, knowing that, I made a stupid mistake for which there was no excuse. I crossed the porch and opened the front door and went into the house.

Some things a man never forgets; some scenes are so deeply burned into his consciousness by the white-hot iron of danger that they linger in his memory until his death. So it was now. Dillingham stood in the middle of the room, his .45 in his hand, the same gun he had laid on the porch the day I fought him, the gun Sarah told Dogbone to take to him.

Sarah sat in the wheel chair behind Dillingham, her face pale, her hands gripping the arms of her chair, but in the quick glance I gave her I saw she wasn't panicky, and that gave me hope.

Maybe Sarah would think of something, anything to give me a chance to go for my gun. But I knew at once that I was reaching for a straw. The slightest squeak of her wheel chair would bring Dillingham around to face her. He would kill her and turn back and shoot me before I could get my gun out of my holster.

All I could think of to say was, ''Well, Gene, I haven't seen you for a long time.''

I stomped snow from my boots; I took off my hat and beat it against my legs, then threw it on the couch. It was all the bravado I could muster, but it was enough to impress Dillingham.

"By God, you're a cool one!" he said.

"Cool, hell!" I said. "I'm cold. It must be twenty below outside."

I took off my coat and tossed it after the hat. Still Dillingham stood as motionless as if he and the gun were carved out of granite. I was doing the only thing I could. If I ignored the gun in his hand, there was a chance he would get rattled, a chance Sarah could produce a miracle, a chance if either Maria or Dogbone was alive and free one of them could do something. But once I provoked him into action, there was no chance at all.

He stood there looking at me, the cocked gun lined on my belly, his square, dark face touched by a sort of stark incredulity. The sheer unexpectedness of my behavior left him confused and uncertain.

Then Sarah said the wrong thing: "Don't be facetious, Will. He's here to murder us. He said that you'd be along before morning, and that he'd wait that long for you if he had to."

Dillingham said: "Yeah, I've been waitin'. Take off your gun belt and lay it on the table—slow."

I obeyed him. "Kathy's all right," I said as calmly as I could. "She tells me you got away with more than $4,000. I'm surprised she'd saved that much."

"That ain't all," Dillingham said with satisfaction. "Me'n Turner done purty well with the Anchor cows this summer." He motioned me back from the table. "I'm goin' away a rich man, Beeson. I'm gonna be as big on some other range as Joe Pardee was on this one." He tapped his chest with the forefinger of his left hand. "That's why I'm cleanin' the widow out. Joe always had some dinero on hand. I reckon she has, too. Where is it?"

Money had become an obsession with him because money, a lot of it, would enable him to achieve Joe Pardee's stature— or so he believed. It explained why he had stayed in the valley all this time, why he had not murdered Sarah and me before now. For the first time I felt that I had a chance; he presented me with the handle I'd been looking for.

"When you find it, will you kill us, Gene?" I asked. "Is that the way we stand?"

He nodded, his heavy lips pressed together so tightly that they pursed out in great bulges below and above his mouth.

"Why should I tell you?" I said.

"You can get it quick and easy," he said, "or slow and hard. Me, I'd rather make it slow and hard. I'm the hairpin who taught the Apaches all they know." He motioned with his left hand toward Sarah's chair. "You've always been sweet on her. If you want to save her some misery, you better talk up."

Dillingham was looking intently at me, paying no attention to Sarah. To him I was the one who represented possible danger, not a paralyzed woman in a wheel chair, and in his judgment I was the one who would lead him to Sarah's money.

"She's got a little, Gene," I said. "I'd find it for you if I knew you'd keep your word."

I had trouble keeping my voice steady. Sarah had stepped out of her chair and was walking toward the desk set against the far wall. I had to keep my eyes on Dillingham, had to keep him looking at me.

I caught little more than a blur from the edge of my vision, but I saw enough to shock me almost as much as Dillingham would have been shocked if he had seen her. She moved with the grace and speed of a woman who had been walking all the time, not with the labored, painful effort I had seen just before she had fallen that day weeks ago.

Dillingham said: "Maybe you don't know I'm gonna keep my word, but if you're smart you'll take a chance I will."

He started to turn his head. I said quickly: "Gene, if I have to beg for my life, I will. You and I rode together a long time. . . ."

"Getting down on your knees ain't gonna do you no good," he said. "I'm done waitin'. Where is it?"

Sarah was at the desk pulling the top drawer open. I said: "In the couch. You know how a woman is. Sarah always did like to sew. She ripped a seam open—"

"All right, all right." He pulled a knife out of his pocket and tossed it on the couch. "Slice it open and give it to me.

If you got a gun over there you're tryin' to get your hands on, you're a goner.''

I didn't want to go to the couch. If I did, I'd be ten feet farther from the table than I was now, ten feet that would cost me seconds. Sarah was fumbling in the drawer. Sweat poured out of me and dripped down my body. I wiped my forehead.

Dillingham laughed. "Come on, come on!"

I shook my head at him. "Use your head, Gene. There isn't much money. Just the $500 I brought from Canon City—"

"Drop your gun, Gene!"

Her voice did not come from where she had been sitting in her wheel chair. She had moved a good twenty feet. He must have been aware of that at once, for he remained motionless a second or so, too surprised to turn. When he did, I lunged toward the table.

She fired, and I heard him yell in pain, heard his gun strike the floor; then I grabbed my holster in one hand and my gun in the other and yanked it free. When I got my eyes on Dillingham, he was bending over, reaching for his .45 with his left hand. I shot him. He fell, and I fired again.

I wasn't myself. I almost pulled the trigger a third time, and then I remembered the day he had killed Al Beam, how he stood over him and put bullet after bullet into the body of a dead man.

I went to him and turned him over with my boot. He was dead. I laid my gun on the table, and swung around to face Sarah, who was walking toward me. She clutched a small single-shot pistol in her right hand, a gun she had used for target shooting before she'd had her accident.

"I shot him in the hand; I shot him in the hand and made him drop his gun!" she said shrilly. "I couldn't make myself kill him, Will. I couldn't!"

She was near me then, her arms reaching for me, and I caught her as she started to fall. She began to cry, her hands feeling my face and the top of my head and the back of my neck, and then she whimpered: "He would have killed us.

He would have killed us. The cooler, Will! He locked María and Dogbone in there.''

She fainted, her head rolling sideways grotesquely. I laid her on the couch and ran through the kitchen to the heavy sawdust-filled door that opened into the cooler. María rushed out, screaming something in Spanish.

"She's all right," I said. "She's on the couch."

Dogbone lay on the floor on his back. I picked him up and felt his head. He'd been knocked cold, just as Kathy Morgan had been. I carried him into the bedroom, the one Joe had used after he'd moved out of Sarah's. When I went into the front room, María was on her knees beside the couch, stroking Sarah's limp hands and talking to her in Spanish.

I told María to take care of both of them. Then I put on my coat and hat and, dragging Dillingham's body behind me, went back into the storm. When I reached the barn, I searched him and found a money belt buckled around his middle just as Turner's had been. I covered the body with a piece of canvas, went to the bunkhouse, and lighted a lamp and built a fire.

I left the money belt on the bunk and took care of my horse. After that I looked around in the dark until I found Dillingham's horse. I put him in the barn, then carried the heavy saddlebags into the bunkhouse. Kathy's money, I thought—money she would have used to buy the Box P if she'd had her way.

I sat down beside the stove and held out my hands to it. The fire was crackling fiercely, and a small cherry-red spot began to show on the side. Though it was hot, so hot I had to move back, I was still cold and shivering. I wondered if I would ever be really warm again.

Chapter Twenty-Nine

I DIDN'T GO TO BED UNTIL DAWN. I HUGGED THE STOVE, smoking one cigarette after another, my thoughts on Sarah. I kept remembering how she had got up from her wheel chair and walked to the desk with the ease and grace of a woman who had never been deprived of the ability to walk. Nela had been right.

I wondered what Sarah would say, what sort of explanation she would make. And I wondered what she would say about selling her half of the ranch. . . .

When I did lie down, I fell into a restless sleep. I didn't wake until nearly noon, when Red and Curly slammed in, cursing the cold and pounding circulation back into their legs and arms.

"Caught the boss in bed!" Red howled in delight.

"And no fire," Curly said disgustedly.

I sat up and rubbed my face, feeling as if I had not slept at all. I said, "I shot, and killed, Gene Dillingham last night."

Red, starting to build a fire, stopped and stared at me. They both stood rigid; then Red muttered, "By God, it was a long time coming."

"He just walk in on you?" Curly asked.

"No," I said, and told them how it had been.

Red got the fire going, and the three of us stood around the stove. Finally Red said: "About Miz Pardee getting up and walking, Will. How do you figure that?"

"I don't know," I said wearily. "I'm not trying to explain it. I'm just telling you what happened. All I know is that if it hadn't happened. I'd be a dead man."

We stood there in silence for a while; then we heard María pounding on the triangle. As we left the bunkhouse Red said: "Sawhill came back with us. Got as far as Alton's Trading Post and decided to wait the storm out."

"He was in a hell of a hurry to get here this morning," Red grumbled. "Talked us into coming with him. Snow was sure bad in the canyon."

The sky had cleared. Because I could see the tracks I'd made going to the bunkhouse the night before, I knew it hadn't snowed much after that. The wind had died down, now, and it was very still and cold, so cold that even a slight noise seemed to run on and on across the frozen snow-draped earth.

María was bending over the big range when we went into the warm kitchen. Sawhill was not in sight. I asked about Sarah, and María said she was in the front room with Sawhill. I asked about Dogbone, and she said he had a headache.

When we finished eating, I said, "I hate to send you boys back into the cold, but there's a couple of chores that's got to be done."

They swore and then grinned, and Red said, "Let's have it."

"One of you will have to take Dillingham's body to town. The other one has to go to Canon City and tell the sheriff."

"Well," Curly said, "I ain't superstitious or nothing, but I don't want to tote no carcass to town. That booger would be sitting right up there in the seat with me before I got to the road."

Red shrugged. "Suits me. I don't care if his ghost sits beside me and holds my hand. I don't hanker to plow through the canyon again."

They left the house, and I went into the front room. Sarah and Sawhill were sitting in rocking chairs in front of the fireplace holding hands. The wheel chair was not in the room. Sawhill rose when he heard me come in, and nodded gravely.

"We were waiting for you, Will," he said. "I'll eat my dinner while Sarah talks to you."

I walked to the fireplace and stood with my back to it. Sarah sat with her head bowed, her hands clasped in her lap. Then, very slowly, she lifted her head and stared at me, and I was shocked by the haggard expression on her face. She looked a dozen years older, a crushed and beaten woman.

"It's not easy for me to say I'm whipped," she said, "but I am. I've never understood how some people can live for such simple things. Joe—happy as long as he kept settlers out of the valley. . . . John—with his silly colony. But you." She shook her head. "You aren't simple-minded."

I expected her to try to explain how she had been able to walk the night before, but that apparently wasn't in her mind at all. She would ignore it, I thought, just as she had ignored so many other things. There was only one world to Sarah Pardee: her world as she wanted to see it, and she would not depart from that world until necessity drove her from it.

But I could not live in her world, and I thought it was the time to make things clear. I said, "I don't know how simple-minded I am, but I can tell you what I want."

"I'd like to hear," she said.

"I want to live on the Box P," I said. "It's home to me. I'm that much like Joe. I can't go off and leave it the way you've told me to. Once I started feeling that half the ranch was mine, I couldn't keep from making plans. Changes that I think would be improvements—"

"Will." She held up a hand. "Will. I should have told you this first. Ben explained it and I understand. You love the Box P. I don't. Besides, you saved my life last night. It's only fair that I leave. I'll sell my half to you. Talk to Ben about it. Any price that he agrees to will satisfy me."

It was as easy as that. I said, "I'll have to see O'Riley, the bank—"

"Don't bother me with all the details," she broke in. "Is that all you want? Are you as single-minded as Joe was?"

"You know what else I want," I said. "I want to bring Nela here as my wife and raise a family and . . ."

"Yes, Will, I know," she said passionately. "Maybe there was a time when Joe felt that way, too, but he began growing in the wrong direction. Don't let it happen to you. I'm going to marry Ben. Give me until tomorrow noon. Dogbone will be able to travel, and María will have my things packed. Then bring your wife here. Sleep with her. Have your children. Grip and hold tight what you want, Will, and never let it go.''

Her voice had risen, almost to a scream. She must have realized it, for she stopped, her hands closed into hard little fists on her lap.

''I wrote to Nela last winter, you know,'' she said, ''and Nela wrote to me, but all that time it never occurred to me you'd fall in love with her. I encouraged her to come with John. If I hadn't, she probably would have stayed in St. Louis. Isn't it funny, Will, how you help to bring about the very thing you don't want to happen?''

She got up and walked to me and put her hands on my shoulders. ''I've just wanted to be loved and cherished, Will. That's all, but I never have been. First my father. My mother died because he dragged her all over the country. I hated him, but I had to go with him. I was cheap help. I cooked and washed for him and patched his clothes. He was like Joe, and like John Mathers: just one idea in his head. He was always going to make a big strike, but he never did.''

She looked at me, the old softness and beauty returning for a moment to her face. This was the Sarah I had loved, but I was sure the Sarah I had known was not the woman who had been Joe Pardee's wife through the last years of his life.

''I'll never forget how you came to me that time down there on the creek,'' she said softly. ''Out of nothing. You did something for me no one else had ever done. You filled a place in my heart that had been empty for as long as I could remember. I bought you with my love, Will. You never knew, but that's the way it was. I owned you, and then when I saw how you felt toward Nela and how she felt toward you . . .'' She swallowed. ''No use to try to tell you what it did to me.''

I backed away a step, but she followed me. ''It will be different with Ben,'' she went on. ''He loves me. Maybe he'll be able to give me what I've needed.'' She put a hand up to the back of my head and tipped it forward. "As long as you've been here, Will, you've never kissed me."

So I kissed her, her hands holding me with possessive strength, and all the time I was afraid that Ben Sawhill would come through the door. Then she wheeled and walked toward the kitchen door, heels clicking sharply on the floor. I turned and went out through the front door, feeling sorry for Ben Sawhill.

I got Dillingham's money belt and saddlebags from the bunkhouse. When I started toward the barn, Red was loading Dillingham's body into the wagon. He stepped into the seat and took the lines. When I reached him, he said: "There was something I aimed to say, Will, but you got to telling how you plugged Dillingham and I plumb forgot. Costello and Brahms and some more—six of 'em, all told—was in Alton's place last night with me and Curly and Sawhill. They'd chased some settlers down ahead of us, you know. O' course, they'd been taking on some of Alton's rotgut, so I don't know how much there was to what they were saying, but they claimed they was gonna clean the West Fork of every clodbuster—"

I started to swear at him, and then I stopped. He said, "Well, now, you've got no call to—"

"I'm sorry, Red." I started toward the corral, on the run. I called back, "I wished you'd told me when you first got here."

He sat there while I threw the saddle on my bay. When I rode out of the yard, he was still sitting there. Then he yelled, "Will, I'll come along if you're gonna need another gun."

"This is a job I've got to do myself," I shouted back at him, and went on down the slope toward the road.

Chapter Thirty

I RODE PAST THE GRIM SKELETON OF MERLE TURNER'S wagon, past the spot where Secore had started his cabin and Turner had been killed, past the places where I had found Mrs. Troy and Mrs. Runyan and had started them downstream toward Carlton. I thought how easy it had been, once Turner was dead. I hadn't considered the possibility that any of them would stay. Joe Pardee always acted on that same basis. No doubt Costello and Brahms had too, but what would they do now?

I couldn't guess. Costello was mostly bluff. Brahms usually followed him. But even a bluffer sometimes finds himself out on a limb and has to make his bluff good. Would Brahms still follow?

I couldn't say. I couldn't decide what Mathers would do, either, beaten and sick as he was. But I had a hunch he would stay here and die if he had to. They wouldn't hurt Nela, but if she saw her father die at their hands would she be able to stay in the valley?

I rode as fast as I could; but there were places where the snow had drifted across the road, and it was all my horse could do to wallow through. I felt I had to stop at Kathy Morgan's place, even though time was all-important.

I ran across the porch and went in without knocking. The house was cold. If Kathy had built a fire, it had gone out. She must have found another bottle. She lay on the couch, and when she heard me come in she lifted herself on one elbow and blinked at me.

"You were wrong," I said. "Sarah's alive, but Dillingham's dead." I threw the heavy saddlebags on the couch. "There's your money!"

She grabbed the saddlebags and hugged them to her breasts. "Poor Gene," she whimpered, and began to cry.

"Sarah's going to marry Ben Sawhill," I said. "She's leaving the valley. I'm buying her half of the ranch. She's out of your reach, Kathy. Do you understand that?"

She cradled the saddlebags in her arms and rocked them back and forth. She said, "Poor Gene. He's dead."

First I shook her, then I slapped her across the face. She started to get up, but fell back, and I saw she was aroused enough to know what I said.

"You've got your money, Kathy," I said slowly. "Sarah is leaving the valley. You can't hurt her any more. Now you're getting out. I'll give you twenty-four hours. If you're not gone . . ."

"I'll be gone," she said. "Nothing to stay for now. Get out of here, Will—get out and leave me alone."

I obeyed. Mounting, I rode across the bridge. When I reached the junction of the road that came up the creek from Alton's Trading Post, I saw that a band of horsemen had come up the canyon and turned west. The nine families that remained were between Carlton and Mathers' place, but I felt certain Costello wouldn't bother them. He'd go after Mathers, knowing that if Mathers left, the others would follow.

I kept on, driven by the knowledge that this was the last job to be done. When it was finished, the uncertainty I had lived with since my fight with Dillingham last spring would be gone. It was the last job and the most important one, because our future depended upon it. If we could not live in peace with other cowmen, neighbors we had known for years, there was no hope for the valley.

When I reached Mathers' cabin, I still had no idea what I would find. Six horses were in front, four with men mounted and two with saddles empty. As soon as I was close enough to recognize the men, I saw that Costello and Brahms were the ones inside. Curly King's father was among the men who waited. The other three were, like him, little ranchers from the south end of the valley.

I spoke when I reined up and stepped down. They greeted me guardedly. I walked through the open door as if I had a right inside, and none of the four raised a hand against me. I stopped just inside the door, motioning for Nela and Scott, who stood against the wall beside the stove, to be silent.

An expression of relief warmed Nela's face as soon as she saw me. I moved out of the doorway and stood with my back to the wall.

Mathers was in bed, his face still bandaged. Costello and Brahms stood facing him, with their backs to me. Costello was pounding a fist into an open palm to emphasize what he was saying. "We've got nothing against you personally, Mathers. It ain't your fault some of your farmers are trying to steal our grass. But as long as any of you are in Easter Valley, it's an invitation for more to come in."

As I listened, I felt a lot easier. I had expected Costello to be far more belligerent than he was. I knew then that I could handle him.

Brahms echoed Costello's words. "We ain't pushing you, Mathers, but we expect you to travel as soon as you're able."

Mathers hadn't moved. He lay on his back much as he had the day before. He said, his voice strong and clear: "If a man exists to perform only the bodily functions that he must do to remain alive, he is not a man in any real sense except the physical. I have long been convinced there is more to life than that. I have searched for the missing parts as long as I can remember, and while I will not say I have found them I will say I am beginning to get their feel. If I left, I would lose it; and I cannot afford to lose something it has taken me half a lifetime to find." He closed his eyes. "Gentlemen, I am not leaving."

Brahms had some admiration for Mathers, I think. Stubborn courage was something he understood and admired. But Costello took a step forward as if he aimed to throw Mathers bodily out of his own cabin. Brahms put an arm in front of him. I couldn't stay out of it any longer.

"You've got one or two things wrong, Irv," I said.

Costello spun around. "When the hell did you sneak in here, Beeson?"

"I didn't sneak, Irv," I answered. "I *walked* in."

Brahms grinned. "Howdy, Will. I hear you done a little moving yourself yesterday."

"A little," I said. "Merle Turner's dead. Last night I shot, and killed, Gene Dillingham. Kathy Morgan is leaving the valley."

They had heard about Turner from Red and Curly, but that was all. They were both knocked back on their heels, Costello especially, because he'd called me a jellyfish, and not fit to rod the ranch Joe Pardee had owned.

There was more to be told, and I thought it was better to say it at once, while they were still off balance. I said: "I'm buying Sarah's half of the Box P. She's moving to Canon City. Maybe you hadn't heard, but Nela and I are married. John Mathers is my father-in-law."

Costello glared at me, his swarthy face red, not knowing what to say. But Brahms let out a whoop and walked across the cabin to where I stood and held out his hand.

"By grab, Will, you sure kept a good thing secret! Congratulations on getting a mighty purty bride." He cuffed me on the chest. "How an ugly maverick like you ever managed it is a mystery to me."

"Me, too," I said. "There's another thing. I bought Delaney out. I figured he wasn't any more of an asset to the community than Kathy Morgan was, feeling the way he does. He wanted to get out, so I accommodated him. I figured my father-in-law could run the store."

Costello still stood there and stared at me, his Adam's apple bobbing up and down in his thick neck and the corners of his mouth working. He'd lost Brahms and he must have known it. I knew I had him because he wasn't a man who could make a stand by himself.

Brahms said: "You've been downright busy, Will. I never cottoned to Delaney, neither. Mathers ought to make a real good counter jumper, hadn't he, Irv?" Brahms winked at me. "I figure we can convert him. Don't you, Will?"

"If I hadn't thought so," I said, "I wouldn't have bought the store. I've been thinking about the nine families that are on the West Fork, Irv. The only cash crop they can count on is hay. Far as I'm concerned, I'd rather pay them to raise it and haul it than piddle around with it myself. I think most of the boys will figure the way I do."

"I would," Brahms said. "What do you say, Irv?"

Costello was backed into a corner now because he was a notoriously poor hay raiser. During at least four of the eight winters I'd been in the valley, he'd been caught short of feed in late winter or early spring, and had come begging to us or Brahms or Dodson.

He said, grudgingly, "Yeah, I guess it'll work out." He cleared his throat. "This puts a different light on things, Mathers, you being Beeson's father-in-law. Naturally, I got no objections to you staying in the valley."

He walked out. Without a word, he stepped into the saddle and started down the road. The four men who had been waiting outside stared after him, uncertain; then they looked at Brahms, who lingered in the doorway, holding out his hand to me again.

"Irv's all right. He jumps in head first. That's his trouble." He shook his head dubiously. "I dunno why he talks me into things like he does,"

"We'll make out all right now," I said. "You'll see, Eric."

"I figure so," he said, and stepped outside. He raised a hand to me as he mounted. "Might as well get along home, boys," he called, and the five of them started down the road slowly, as if they were in no hurry to catch up with Costello.

What could have been a shooting scrape had sputtered out, and I suspected Costello was still trying to figure out how it had happened. Nela could hold back no longer. She ran to me. "Will, Will," she said, "I don't know what they would have done if you hadn't come!" She kissed me, and I held her close for a long moment.

Nela drew back and looked at me questiongly. "Is it true? What you said about buying Sarah's half of the Box P."

"True as gospel," I said. "We've got to give her until

tomorrow noon; then you move in, and from then on you're running it. The work's all yours, too, including cooking for three men."

"I'm not afraid of the work, Will," she said. "It was Sarah."

We walked to Mathers' bedside, my arm around Nela's waist. I said, "I didn't intend to spring the store thing on you this way, but it seemed the best way to do it, with Costello here." I dropped Dillingham's money belt on the bed. "There's the rest of your cow money. At least it isn't all lost. How about the store? Will you take it?"

"I'll be glad to," he answered. "I want to stay in the valley, and maybe the store is where I belong. I've had a lot of time to think lately. I talked too big and dreamed too big, and I got flattened out. But I don't feel as bad as I did. We did accomplish something in bringing nine families here. It looks as if they have every chance of staying and being happy and prosperous, thanks to you."

"That what you meant about finding what you were searching for?"

"Partly," he said, "but there's something else. My trouble was, I got my eyes off the stars I'd been looking at. Since I've been lying here I've rediscovered a simple truth I should never have forgotten. You don't build a Great Tomorrow unless a lot of Great Todays have gone before."

"Why," I said, "I guess that's right."

Nela said briskly, "I'll get supper started."

She crossed the room to the stove. I followed her. I said, "Nela, our troubles aren't over."

She wrinkled her nose at me. "Do you think I'm the kind of woman who believes you get married and live happily ever after? Well, I'm not. I'll work for you and I'll have your children and I'll always love you; but I've got an awful temper, and one of these days you'll find that out."

I laughed. I just couldn't help it. I felt good all the way through.

"Well, now," I said, "I'll bet I will."

SPEND YOUR LEISURE MOMENTS WITH US.

Hundreds of exciting titles to choose from—something for everyone's taste in fine books: breathtaking historical romance, chilling horror, spine-tingling suspense, taut medical thrillers, involving mysteries, action-packed men's adventure and wild Westerns.

SEND FOR A FREE CATALOGUE TODAY!

Leisure Books
Attn: Customer Service Department
276 5th Avenue. New York. NY 10001